coffee, kids, and a kidnapping

A CHARLOTTE RITTER MYSTERY
ALYSSA HELTON

This book is dedicated to my three amazing children. They inspire me to keep fighting, keep moving forward, and to keep reaching for the stars. I love you more than coffee!

chapter one

H *onk! Honk!*
     "Mom, the light's green! Go!" squealed my thirteen year old daughter.

"I can, believe it or not, see colors. It's this van. It's twelve years old. It doesn't take off at break-neck speed."

"It's just that if I'm late for practice, I have to run the fence."

"Coach Jim will understand."

"If I have good behavior, I get a soda right?" came a voice from the far back seat of the van.

"Yes, Tommy. Good behavior while your sister practices softball, and you get a green Sprite." I nodded, trying not to get to flustered.

We pulled into the ballfield parking lot with three minutes to spare. Carrie jumped out and ran to join her team. All that worry about running…

Tommy held onto my arm as we walked to the stands. He was fifteen and nearly six feet tall, but autism didn't allow him to be a typical teenager. He wiggled his fingers in front of his face and scripted lines from Monsters, Inc.

"I love you, schmoozy poo!" he said, giggling.

Finding a spot on the end of a row, I sat down while Tommy paced back and forth in the grass behind the dugout. He wore headphones connected to an older iPod Touch that we got for a great deal on Ebay. He sat and watched YouTube videos of his favorite shows: Rugrats, Spongebob, Annoying Orange and anything by Pixar. Thank God the park had Wi-Fi.

The bleachers were aluminum and had gotten scorching hot in the Florida sun. Whoever's idea it was to have metal seats and no awning to cover them ought to be strung up by his heels. I spread out a blanket to sat on it and took a sip of my hazelnut coffee I'd brought from home.

"Carrie, do you have water?" I yelled towards the dugout.

"Yeah, Mom! I grabbed a bottle out of the cooler!"

She played for the Pirates and they wore black baseball pants and black shirts with black hats. Did I mention the Florida sun? I worried about her dehydrating or at least getting overheated. Being a blonde, she had a fair complexion.

"Everybody out on the field! Let's move!" Coach Jim shouted in gruff tone.

The girls poured out onto the field and get into position. Carrie was playing shortstop for the first time this season, and she was ready for action. Knees bent. Eyes on the batter. The ball was hit! A grounder... heading right for Carrie! She ran forward, scooped up the ball and hurled it to first. Out!

"Good job, ladies! Stay alert in the outfield!" Coach Jim said clapping his hands and almost cracking a smile.

Another hit and it was a pop fly toward center field. No one called it and it landed between two outfielders.

"What was that? You gotta call it, dirt bags! Call it! What'd I say?" He shouted, no longer clapping.

The girls answered back in unison, "Call it!"

Sure, Coach Jim sounded a bit rough; calling them dirt bags and all, but, the girls knew he was really just a big teddy bear and they loved him. He'd call them by the wrong names and pretend to have a heart attack when they'd screw up. But, he also drilled them on good defense and had no qualms benching them if their grades dropped. He and his wife treated the team like their own kids, only a little less strict.

"Maymay! It's gone! They took it off forever!" Tommy came crying. It sounded like the end of the world was eminent.

I looked at the iPod and saw that it was offline. "We just have to connect to the Wi-Fi again, buddy. I can fix it," I assured him.

A few seconds later, with a whispered prayer and a quick reconnect, he was back to watching his videos.

My oldest son, Joseph—a senior in high school—had stayed home to do homework. I decided to call and check on his progress.

"Hey, Mom. I'm working. I promise." He said as soon as he answered the phone.

"Hello to you, too. I was just checking in. How's it going?"

His voice turned pitiful. "Painfully slow. This essay is a beast. And I'm starving."

"You're always starving. I've got supper in the crock pot. Don't touch it! Wait 'til we get home." I told him with my best stern mom inflection.

"Yes, ma'am. I'm gonna grab a soda and get back to writing."

"Alright. Just be thankful you have the internet to do your research. When I was in school—"

"Yeah, I know. You had to go through catalog cards and microfiche, spend days at the library, yada, yada, blah, blah, blah."

"I could always break out the encyclopedias," I quipped.

"That's alright. I'm thankful, really. Completely filled with gratitude for how easy I have it."

"That's my boy. I'll text you when we leave the park."

I know what you're thinking. How sarcastic. How rude. Well, sarcastic, yes. But, rude? Never. Joseph was as good a kid as you could find anywhere. Sarcasm is our love language. Same with Carrie. The only one who didn't completely grasp that concept was Tommy. Another byproduct of autism.

It was finally Carrie's turn at bat. The ball went right over the plate. Strike! Another ball went right through the zone. Strike 2! On the third pitch she swung her new bat and to everyone's surprise she hit a double. I cheered and Tommy stopped watching videos long enough to clap his hands for her. Later in the practice, she caught a pop fly but I missed it because I was watching for Tommy to walk back from the bathroom. That had always been one of the toughest parts about being a single parent; especially having a special needs child. Only having one set of eyes, one set of ears and two arms. I couldn't be everywhere I needed to be nor could I do everything I needed to do. Fortunately, the kids were old enough to realize that I did my best.

"Mom, did you see my catch?" she asked as we're walking towards the van after practice.

"I saw the second one. Just heard about the first one. Sorry. Tommy had to use the restroom."

"No worries! At least you saw one. And next Saturday during our first game, there'll be more for you to see!"

"Better be!"

We arrived home and the smell of barbecue chicken carried me through the front door like Bugs Bunny in one of those cartoons, riding a wave of a delicious smell. I dished out the pulled chicken and its tangy sauce over piles of rice because, as my kids knew well, I was the chicken and rice queen.

"Chicken and rice version sixty-four," I announced.

The kids laughed and grabbed plates. Tommy sat down to his place at the table with four used soda cans now filled with water.

"Mom, why does he do this? What is with this soda obsession?" asked Carrie, who worried about her brothers like a mother hen.

"I'll give you the only answer I know to give. Because autism. We may never know why he does what he does."

"Red Coka Coley has been fighting with green Sprite so he's in time-out," Tommy explained as he turned his Coke can around.

"Oh." replied Joseph. "Okay then. So, what's for dessert?"

"We just sat down to eat supper!" I shouted in joking exasperation.

"I know. I'm just thinkin' ahead." He explained as he took a bite of chicken.

"Popsicles in the freezer in the garage, watermelon in this fridge or there's a couple cookies left from the weekend…I think. Did you get that essay completed?"

"Yep," he replied in between bites. "And I found seven more images for my laptop wallpaper."

Joseph's autism manifested as Asperger's. He was very high functioning; in honors classes in school, tested mid-level in his grade. But, there were quirks. Making lists, listening to music and finding images from his favorite movies and TV shows for his computer were his favorite activities. For example, just that morning he'd shared with me his list of his twenty-five favorite male actors of the big screen.

"Can't wait to see them," I told him, trying my best to seem excited.

Not that I didn't like to see what he was interested in; I did. But, it had been a long day and I was tired. Nevertheless, I ate my watermelon while looking at pictures from Inception and Alien and discussing the evolution of special effect technology.

The kids helped me by rinsing their dishes and placing them in the dishwasher while I wiped down the counters. Then my phone rang. It was my boss, Dan Baker, a family law attorney who specialized in custody cases and adoptions. I was his research assistant. My occupation bugged my kids to no end because I was one of the few parents who was actually more tech-savvy than the average teenager. Not with social media, but general internet searches and government documents. If you gave me a name I could find every available document on that person and their relatives going back five generations.

"Hello, boss," I answered.

"Good evening, Charlotte. Sorry to bother you at home. I just remembered I'll be in late tomorrow because I have to be in court, and I left that Williams file on my desk. Thought you might need it and would be wondering where it was."

"Thanks for the heads up. I do have a couple more things to finish up with that case. I brought home the

Murphy files to review tonight so I can get a head start in the morning." I said.

"Terrific. I'll see you and Cole around lunch time."

Hanging up the phone, I grabbed the dish towel and snapped it towards Carrie.

"Aaah! What's that for?"

"For sneaking a second cookie! Did you really think I wouldn't see that?"

She and Joseph started laughing and running around the house while I chased them with the towel. Tommy grabbed his headphones and ran upstairs to escape our nonsense. It lasted about ten minutes.

"Alright, enough of that. I've got some work to do, and I'm sure you've got homework—reading or studying or something?" I questioned Carrie.

"Just a couple chapters to read. Won't take me long. You've got more homework than we do! Why are you always bringing work home?"

"I honestly get more research done here at home. At the office, there's so many distractions like phone calls, finished cases to file away, paperwork for court. If I wait 'til you all go to bed, I can sit at my desk with peace and quiet and actually focus."

"I get that. As long as you're researching for work and not, oh you know, running a background check on my softball coach…or the boy that asked me to the school dance!"

"That only happened once and technically I didn't check his background. I checked his father's."

She looked at me through squinty eyes and wrinkled her nose. "Same difference!"

"Go read a book," I ordered, waving her off to her room. "I've got laundry to do before I have to tuck Tommy in."

I finally got everyone settled into their rooms and told goodnight. Tommy's ritual was no less than six steps: a hug, a kiss, him saying "goodnight," me saying "goodnight," him saying "be good," and me saying, "you, too." It had always been our thing. Yes, sometimes it felt like a drudgery, but I tried to remember it was something he needed to do in order to feel relaxed enough for bed. It was something he only did with me, and it was sweet.

Sipping my evening tea, I start scanning pages in the file for our new adoption case. The Murphys had been the foster parents for eight year old Maddox since he was three. My job was to find any relatives that might pose a threat to the adoption. A lot of times, these relatives wanted nothing to do with raising a child that isn't their own. Otherwise, the kid would have been placed with them for foster care. Occasionally, however, a relative would catch wind of an upcoming adoption and cause an uproar; either because they felt the child should remain in the family or they thought they'd get financial benefits if they took custody. In this case, Maddox's parents were both killed when the meth lab they were running exploded. No living grandparents. No siblings. No one coming forward to claim this little boy. No one, that is, except the Murphys.

My eyes were so heavy, I could barely read any of the documents—no matter how hard I stared. I gave up and stuck the file in my bag by the back door. Grabbing a pen, I wrote a note to remind the boys to take showers the next morning and taped it to the fridge. I knew they'd see it if they beat me to the kitchen for breakfast.

The next day was Sunday and with church not starting 'til ten thirty meant I'd get to sleep in. Hallelujah!

chapter two

"Maymay, I need a towel!" hollered Tommy.

I stuck my head out from the covers and grabbed my phone. I could've slept another ten minutes. Why wasn't he getting a towel from the closet? Oh, yeah. They were still in the dryer.

"Maymay, did you hear me?" came another frantic shout.

"Yes, Tommy, I'm coming!"

Feeling part thankful that he saw the note about showering and part aggravated that I missed out on ten minutes, I threw on my robe and left the comfort of my room. It was bright in the hallway because Tommy seemed to think all the lights needed to be on once he was awake.

"Go ahead and get in the shower. I'll bring you a towel and put it by the sink," I told him.

Slowly maneuvering down the stairs, I smelled something familiar.

"Do I smell coffee?"

"Yeah, I made you some," said Carrie with a smile. "I heard Tommy yelling for you and figured you'd need it."

"That's why you're my favorite," I joked.

"Hey, I'm sitting right here," Joseph mumbled with a mouth full of waffle.

"You're my favorite, too," I told him.

"You have two favorites?" he asked, finally swallowing.

"I have three. You have seven favorite movies based on comic books, so don't judge me."

Joseph laughed and turned his attention back to the waffles. I sipped my coffee and grabbed a towel from the dryer.

"If anyone needs a towel, just grab one from here. I'll fold them later…after church. Be sure to put your dishes in the dishwasher."

"Yes, ma'am," Carrie said, walking away with a piece of turkey bacon in one hand a cup of iced tea in the other. "I'm gonna start getting ready."

"We don't have to leave for two hours," I reminded her.

"I know."

Joseph shook his head. "Must be a girl thing."

"Says the boy who takes a forty minute shower."

"Yeah, but I can be dressed and ready in five minutes!"

I took Tommy the towel and retreated to my room with my coffee so I could read my devotional. It was about patience and it quoted Ephesians 4:2: "Be always humble, gentle and patient. Show your love by being tolerant with one another." Great. This one was really stepping on my toes. I could be patient with my kids, especially Tommy, as I understood the need for it. But patience with other people? That's a different story. I said a quick prayer, asking God for help with this particular matter and started getting dressed for church.

Needing to leave no later than ten fifteen, I started calling the kids downstairs at…ten fifteen.

"Guys, let's go! We've gotta leave now!"

"Coming!" shouted Carrie from somewhere. I wasn't sure where exactly.

"Five seconds!" yelled Joseph.

"Holy roosters! I can't find my shoes!" Tommy ranted.

Five minutes later (and ten minutes late) we ran to the van and peeled out of the driveway at warp speed. Thankfully, Tommy's shoes had been found by the back door before we started our frantic SWAT team style, tear-the-house-apart search.

I parked in outer Mongolia and the four of us speed-walked to the church doors. Carrie and Joseph took Tommy to his special needs Sunday school class before they joined the youth group in the chapel. Grateful that it wasn't my Sunday to sing with the praise team, I took a bulletin from Sister Agnes and looked for an empty seat in the back. The music had begun, everyone was standing and the lights were dimmed so that was hard to see an available place to sit.

"There you are! I was beginning to think you weren't coming," Momma Pat whispered in my ear as she gave me a hug.

Mama Pat was a member of the group I affectionately referred to as the Gaggle of Grannies. This group of four older women had taken me under their wing. Like the time they caught wind that I had asked a man for his email address. The Grannies descended on me with loving rebuke for being so forward. Little did they realize he was one of Carrie's softball coaches. Even when they were made aware of their error, they took it upon themselves to share with me the proper etiquette they had been taught "back in the days of decency." Of course, I once called an ambulance when I spotted seventy-six year old Mammaw Sellers prostrate on the floor through her living room window. She had actually been resting between yoga poses. My bad. Anyway, they loved me and I loved them and we looked out for each other…whether we liked it or not.

"We're late because Tommy couldn't find his shoes," I whispered back. "Catch you after service."

I found an aisle seat just a couple rows up from the very back and slid in as the first song ended. Worship service was my reprieve from everything else in life. It took a while to find a place that could accommodate Tommy. I felt so blessed to have a special needs ministry that is so well-equipped and well-trained that I could enter into worship without the anxiety of wondering how soon my number would pop up on the screen because I needed to rescue some poor Sunday school teacher from one of Tommy's meltdowns.

Standing there with my arms lifted, singing "You're My Healer," it occurred to me how God had healed me not just physically but emotionally over the previous two years. The kids and I had found our place, our routine, our tribe. Nothing like counting your blessings to open up those tear ducts.

Pastor Smith admonished us to display fruits of the Spirit as he dismissed us from service. Turning to leave, I walked straight into Granny. The second oldest of the Gaggle at eighty-two, Granny was kind of the leader and Momma Pat's mother. She was known for her homemade cookies and for pulling loose teeth for practically every child in the church. I'd seen parents bring in crying kids who magically stood still for Granny to pull their teeth. If ever there was a Spiritual gift, this was Granny's.

"I'm glad I ran into you. I didn't see you before church."

"We came in late. Tommy and his shoes."

"Again?"

"Keeping up with shoes is a work in progress."

"It's a man thing. My late husband, God rest him, couldn't find anything. He could be looking straight at it and still ask me where it was. Here, I made Carrie some peanut butter cookies. She said they're a good snack when she's playing ball."

"You spoil her."

"I do not. She's the sweetest child. Not a brat at all. That's proof she ain't spoiled."

The other Grannies trotted up alongside us. This included Mammaw Sellers (who did yoga, as I mentioned before) and Little Momma who was the tiniest African American woman I'd ever seen and wore the biggest, fanciest hats I'd ever seen…in all colors.

"Hey, Little Momma, is that a new hat? Sure is pretty."

"Honey, Jesus picked this one out for me to wear today. Been sittin' in my closet for months and this mornin' when I was praying, I asked Him which hat to wear and this one fell off the shelf! Hallelujah!"

Each of the Grannies gave me a squeeze before I excused myself to get the kids home for lunch. Those beloved old women left me with a box of cookies, two new handkerchiefs (with embroidered flowers), a recipe for blackberry cobbler and a roll of mints.

One thing I always loved about using a crockpot was walking in the door and being welcomed home by the smell of something delicious. The chicken and dumplins I had started this morning made our house smell like

Cracker Barrel. I'm not a spectacular cook, but I can hold my own. I was feeling quite pleased with myself until I remembered how picky kids can be.

"I'm gonna make myself a salad. Anyone else want one?" offered Carrie.

"You're not even going to try my chicken and dumplins?" I asked, insulted.

"Sorry, Mom. Dumplins are just…gross."

"Whatever. More for me!" exclaimed Joseph. At least one kid knew good food when he smelled it.

"Tommy, you want some lunch?" I asked knowing full-well he'd snacked too much during Sunday school to be hungry.

"I'll get some when I'm ready," he replied, running towards his room and his allotted computer time.

Joseph and I sat down to eat and started a discussion about how Christians need to make better quality movies and stop being so cheesy. That lead to him rambling on about directors and screenwriters so much that I grabbed my work files to read through while he talked. He'd always been okay with this. Joseph had come to the realization that he could carry on a one-sided conversation for quite some time. We had an understanding. He'd talk to his heart's content; I'd nod and say things like "yeah" and "uh-huh" while doing something else. We were good with this arrangement.

"It boils down to writing. The quality just isn't there," he surmised.

"Maybe. I do think sometimes they try too hard to convey a certain message," I added while digging in my purse for my glasses.

He kept going and opened the Murphy file. I scanned the list of Maddox's relatives between bites of dumplins and sips of sweet tea. The only ones who hadn't been checked off the list were an aunt (his mother's sister) and cousin who went missing a few months before. The aunt's husband had been contacted via certified letter, signed the paperwork and submitted it without a formal interview. I wondered what happened to his wife and daughter. The notion occurred to me that she may have escaped to a women's shelter. If that was the case, she could've still sought custody of Maddox later on. I jotted down a note to see if I could locate her and tie-up that lose end. It pays to be thorough.

"And that's why I think they could learn from Hollywood...how to convey a message with subtlety. It's done all the time!" Joseph stated, completing his rant.

"Agreed. Although I think it's as much sneakiness as it is subtlety."

"Ooooh. You're right! Are Christians allowed to be sneaky?"

"Read the story of Gideon's attack on the enemy. Sneakiness is most certainly allowed."

Carrie finally sat beside me with her practically gourmet salad.

"I have to admit, that looks really good," I confessed.

"I went all out. Bean sprouts, bacon bits, extra cheese... want a bite?"

"No, thanks. I'll do good to finish what I've got."

"Eyes bigger than your stomach?" She asked grinning.

"Yep."

"What's for dessert?" Joseph asked as he rinsed his bowl before placing it in the dishwasher.

"Dessert? Really? You know you don't have to have dessert with every single meal."

He looked at me like I had three heads or something.

"I digress. I think there's popsicles in the freezer." I said...slightly deflated.

"That'll work." He grabbed one and plopped back down at the table.

"Maymay, I can eat now," announced Tommy, entering the kitchen.

"There's chicken and dumplins. You can put it in the bowl yourself."

Tommy leaned over the crockpot and took a whiff. Then with no visible emotion he said, "No, thanks. I must have peanut butter and jelly?"

I sighed and roll my eyes like a punk teenager.

"I'll help him," Joseph said, heading towards the pantry.

"Thanks, buddy. I've got some work to do. Looks like I need to track down a missing person for this adoption case."

"Leave your bowl. We'll load the washer," Carrie offered.

Good kids. I've got such good kids.

Having changed into comfy loungewear, i.e. yoga pants and a baggy t-shirt, I settled at my desk to do some research. The usual first step is to check the obvious like social media accounts and public records in our county as well as neighboring counties. A lot of times, I found that the people no one else can seem to locate are still within fifty miles of their last known address. But, my first step in this case was to check the background on this uncle. My gut feeling told me that something was up with him, and sure enough…I found a restraining order filed against him along with an arrest record that included assault and drunken disorderly. This confirmed my idea that the aunt could have taken refuge in a shelter for abused women. It was certainly a possibility and one worth looking into.

"Maymay!" Tommy yelled from the living room. "The VCR isn't working and—"

"I'm coming! Hold on!" I yelled back, practically running to open my bedroom door.

"I put the video in but it's just fuzzy and there's no sound," he frantically explained.

"Maybe the channel got changed. I'll take a look."

Sure enough, someone had hit the input button on the remote so that the video wouldn't show on the television screen. Thankfully, I had learned to troubleshoot these kind of problems back when Tommy was little. Of course, that was after I spent years of panicking as much as he did because I couldn't resolve whatever it was that had gotten him upset.

"Okay, buddy. It's working now."

"Thanks, Maymay. You're the best."

"I try. Now, I need to get some work done. You alright?"

"Yep. Be good!" he called out to me as I walk out of the room.

"You, too!" I replied.

Back at my desk, I sat down to look over this guy's police record.

Knock. Knock.

"Hey, Mom? I just remembered I have this math homework, and I'm not really sure how to do it. The instructions are confusing."

Sigh. "Okay, honey. Take it to the kitchen table and I'll be right there. I've just got to save some of this information for work tomorrow."

And, that's how it typically goes, right? As soon as I comment on how much work I get done at home, I don't get any done at all.

chapter three

You know how sometimes you wake up naturally, thinking it's the middle of the night and that you'll be able to fall back to sleep for a few hours; only to realize by the blurry numbers on your cell phone that in just two minutes your alarm will sound? Yeah. I hate that, too. I know Mondays get a bad rep, but I usually didn't mind them. Our weekly routine remained fairly consistent compared to our weekends. I liked routine. I also liked being punctual.

"Kids, get a move on! I'm gonna quit feeding ya'll big breakfasts if it's gonna make you move this slow!" I threatened.

"I'm coming! Just gotta grab my library book," yelled Joseph from his room.

"Two minutes! I'm trying to do my hair," complained Carrie.

"I'm ready, Maymay," said a proud Tommy, standing at the door with his backpack on, shoes tied and noise-cancelling headphones in hand.

I have to admit I was proud too and quite surprised. I gave him a quick hug then we all ran out the door with me rattling off lists of things they had best have with them: phones, lunch or lunch money, permission slips, homework, etc. While driving down the road, Carrie read us our family devotional and we prayed for safety and guidance throughout the day. It wasn't a relaxed, sit-down devotion time like I would have preferred, but it got the job done. God sees all the stuff I have to do. He gets it.

Joseph and Tommy were let off at the high school, Carrie exited the vehicle a block away from the middle school, and I got to work fifteen minutes early. Without my coffee.

"Where's my coffee?" I questioned myself aloud, alone in the van. Images of my previous actions for the morning filled my head. Breakfast. Gathering files. Helping Tommy brush his teeth. Placing my coffee in the microwave. Taking the coffee ou…oh…wait…yep… that's where it was. Knowing it could quite possibly make me late, I committed to taking the risk of driving to the McDonald's just down the road. Coffee is a necessity.

Thanks to the seven cars in line at the drive-thru, I stepped into work at precisely nine o'clock.

"You're late," Cole, my co-worker remarked in shock. "I mean, not really. You're never late. Usually, you're here for half an hour before anyone else. Something happen?"

"Forgot my coffee at home."

Cole shook his head, understanding. "I knew it had to be some kind of emergency."

Cole Lee was the paralegal at the law office, but most people didn't believe me when I introduce him. At six foot four, two-hundred and forty pounds with a shiny bald head and a couple of noticeable tattoos, well…he was intimidating. That tough façade came in handy when he moonlighted as a bouncer at a local nightclub. As a divorced dad with child support to pay, he said having the extra job was a must.

"I knew you'd understand. Us coffee addicts got to stick together," I teased.

"Worked the club last night," Cole explained, holding an extra-large cup from Starbucks.

"No judgment here. But, hey, once you're more awake, I've got something to show you on this Murphy adoption."

"I'm awake. This cup is half empty already. What'cha got?"

We stepped into my office which was once the walk-in closet for our house-turned-lawyer's office and I dug the files out of my bag.

"I printed some stuff out last night that I found online. Maddox has this uncle that's already signed-off relinquishing any rights he may have. But, this uncle's wife, Amber, is Maddox's mother's sister. She'd have some rights to custody but she's missing, along with her daughter Lily."

"What are police saying?"

"I haven't talked to them yet. But, Amber filed for a restraining order against Randy which suggests she may have left for a women's shelter for safety."

"So, you're thinking you should find her and get her to sign-off on Maddox's adoption before she comes out of hiding and messes things up."

"Exactly."

Cole stood there, leaning against the door frame, sipping his coffee.

"Well?" I asked. "You think I'm right? I should find her. Don't you think so?"

He rubbed his chin while obviously in deep thought.

"Yeah, you should. But," he added, "you need to be careful. This Randy dude could be dangerous. There's another scenario you either didn't think of or just didn't want to include."

"What's that?"

"That Maddox's aunt didn't escape," he replied with one eyebrow raised.

"Well, she didn't just vanish."

"Charlotte," Cole said with a sigh. "I know she didn't vanish. This abusive husband of hers could've gotten out of control."

I finally got his hint. "Oh! You think he could've killed her?"

Cole shrugged. "Don't act like the thought hadn't crossed your mind. You know full well that it's a possibility. Talk to the police and do some online digging like you usually do. But, don't try talking to this guy yourself, okay? He could be bad news."

"What bad news?" Mr. Baker, my boss, asked while walking through the door; stumbling into our conversation.

"Maddox's uncle. I think the aunt may be at a women's shelter and I need to ensure she can't file for rights and interfere with the adoption."

"The aunt that's listed as missing? Police have been searching for her with no luck. Wouldn't a shelter have to report her whereabouts?"

"Not all of them do. It's worth looking into."

Mr. Baker thought silently for a moment, making a strange face as he twisted his mouth and glanced toward the ceiling.

"Alright. Look into it, but don't get too involved," he said. He walked to his office and closed the door.

"Did you hear that?" Cole asked me with that eyebrow raised again. "Don't get too involved."

"Why do you two keep pullin' on the reins? I'm just doing my job."

"And you do it exceptionally well. But, you could bog yourself down in so much research trying to find this woman that you delay the adoption for no reason. I know you. You'll consider this search a personal mission."

Waving him off, I turned on my heel and went back to my desk. He thought he knew me…phooey. I sat down and started bringing up documents and websites to begin my search. "I bet I have this woman found by lunch." I thought to myself. Did I mention my humility?

Yeah, okay, lunchtime came and went and still no Aunt Amber or cousin Lily. I'd gone through registries and databases. I called every women's shelter within a fifty-mile radius and asked that they have Amber get in touch with me concerning her nephew. I called police departments and hospitals. Nothing. I was beginning to doubt my abilities as a researcher. Having reached the point of self-doubt and complete frustration, there was only one thing left to do…text my bestie.

Su Montgomery and I had known each other since college, but had just reconnected via Facebook a couple of years before. Both of us being autism moms, our friendship had flourished well beyond anything we had while sitting in our college chorale rehearsals. But, that's a story for another time. Su lived in Mississippi and we stayed in touch through texts and emails. Neither of us were really phone-talkers (unless it was business) and you know how kids are when a mom gets on the phone. Anyway, I texted her my dilemma.

Doubting myself. Can't find this woman. Feel like she's hiding. Maybe in danger? Maybe dead! Ugh. My skills are lacking on this one.

A minute later, I heard my phone notification sounding over and over again. Six texts.

You are a very capable woman but you can't do everything. And if she's dead (God forbid!), you certainly can't find her through standard research techniques. Center yourself and pray and maybe...let it go?

First of all, yes we knew texting should be abbreviated and filled with slang. We didn't roll that way other than the occasional *LOL* and an overload of emoticons. Second of all, I knew I couldn't do everything. I didn't want to do everything. I just wanted to find this woman! I felt compelled to find her. So, taking Su's advice, I centered myself and prayed; asking God for guidance. This case was starting to raise my blood pressure.

A while later, Mr. Baker stood at my desk taking large bites of a loaded hotdog from Mustard's Last Stand, a local favorite that's just down the road.

"Any word on that aunt?" he asked with a bite still in his mouth and mustard on his chin.

"No," I admitted with disdain. "I put in a request to speak to the Palm Bay police officer who interviewed Randy, the uncle. I'm hoping he might give me a lead. Otherwise, it's a dead end."

"Well, if he doesn't have any information, just drop it. We need to start processing paperwork with the court and get this adoption done."

"Yes, sir. Oh, and sir, you have mustard right here," I motioned with my hand.

"Thanks." He said as he wiped his chin with a napkin. "The best food is the messiest!"

"You sound like Tommy," I joked.

My phone rang and I answered with anticipation. "Charlotte Ritter, researcher for Dan Baker attorney at law."

A man with a deep and authoritative voice responded. "Miss Ritter? This is Sergeant Paul Atwood. I got a message that you called about Randy Tipton."

"Yes, I did. Thank you for returning my call. I'm actually looking for his estranged wife, Amber, in regards to a pending adoption of her nephew. I was hoping that since you interviewed Mr. Tipton, you might have a lead for me as to her whereabouts."

"I spoke with him a few times, and I can tell you two things. One, he knows where she is and two, he can't be trusted. Problem is, I don't have any real evidence to pursue him. He's simply a person of interest in an on-going investigation."

"My thoughts were that she went to a shelter to escape his abuse."

"We looked into that. Problem is, Mr. Tipton has a couple of buddies on the force. If Mrs. Tipton told the shelter this information, it's possible they would hide her location from us."

"That's impeding an investigation!"

"Well, it'd be for her safety. I'm assuming you didn't find her at any of the local shelters."

"No. I was really hoping you could point me in the right direction."

"Wish I could. I'm afraid the only one who could do that is Randy Tipton himself. But, he ain't likely to."

I thanked the sergeant and hung up, severely disappointed. My expression must be revealing because Cole handed me a piece of his Dove chocolate stash.

"No leads?' he asked. His voice was gentle and calm. Guess he was trying to console me or something. He was sweet.

"Nope. Well…the only lead is Randy Tipton, but he's apparently not sharing information. Wish I could talk to him."

"Think you could be more persuasive than police officers and attorneys?"

I give him the same look I give my kids when they question me. "I think it's possible. He wouldn't see me as a threat. Might let some info slip."

Cole laughed and almost choked on his chocolate. "You've been watching too much television."

Ignoring his continuous snickering (so much for consoling), I picked up the phone and called Tiffany Doyle, Maddox's Guardian ad Litem. You might be wondering what on earth that is. Well, the Guardian ad Litem (GAL) program was the brainchild of a judge in the Seattle juvenile court who was concerned about the lack of information and representation of children in cases of abuse and neglect. GAL was formed in 1977 to give these children an assigned volunteer who would be their voice and would present the child's best interest to the court. Today there are a thousand programs in forty-nine states that have helped over two-hundred-thousand children.

Tiffany was the volunteer assigned to Maddox through GAL, and she knew him better than almost anyone. She was in constant contact with his teachers, doctors, therapists and foster family. Maddox went with Tiffany twice a month for a fun outing where he was comfortable talking and could really open up. She supported the Murphys adopting Maddox. I felt obligated to let her know what was going on.

"Hey, Tiffany, it's Charlotte. There's a situation I want to bring to your attention."

"Uh-oh. That doesn't sound good."

"I'm sure everything is gonna go smoothly. I don't want you to worry. It's just that I'm looking into Maddox's aunt Amber, the one that went missing with her daughter. She may have ran-off to escape her abusive husband. My goal is to locate her and get her to sign-off on the adoption so that she doesn't show up down the road and decide she wants custody."

"I was told that her wanting him was highly unlikely… even if you find her."

"That may be true. My job is to tie up all these loose ends; the ones that can lead to upheaval later on. I feel compelled to follow this through and rule her out as a next of kin with possible rights to custody."

"I understand. You're being thorough. I appreciate that. You'll keep me posted, then?"

"Absolutely. Maddox still doing okay?"

"He's great. He loves his new family. They're all happy."

"Wonderful. I want them to stay happy."

"I hear you. Check in with me if you find his aunt. Thank you for going the extra mile."

chapter four

Monday nights meant two things in the Ritter household: Chinese take-out and a cheesy movie. We chose General Tso's chicken and fried rice from our local Panda Express and turned on Mystery Science Theater 3000 on Netflix. Sometimes Tommy would join us, but most of the time he chose to ignore us and watched something on his iPad with headphones. This night was one of those nights.

"Tommy, this movie is really funny and it has dinosaurs in it," Carrie told him.

"No, thanks," he replied, remembering to use his manners. "I've got Veggie Tales episodes that need me."

Joseph rolled his eyes. "Does this mean you're gonna sing along?"

"Of course it does," Tommy admitted without hesitation.

"Okay, then if you want to sing along you need to either be in another room or just hum quietly. We are wanting to watch a movie," I informed him.

"You're going to watch that silly show with the robots?" He asked.

"Yes. And the movie they're making fun of has dinosaurs. Sure you don't want to join us?"

"I'm sure. Come on, Coca Coley, let's go eat and we can watch 'Are You My Neighbor.'" Tommy told his drink as he walked to the dining table where his iPad and Chinese food awaited him.

The rest of us piled on the couch holding our plates and forks and resting our feet on the coffee table. My grandmother would not have approved. The episode started just as I took my first bite and we already began to hear Tommy humming in the background. Quite the dilemma. Do we send him to another room and feel guilty like we've shunned him or something? Or do we tolerate the humming and turn up the volume a little to compensate? Joseph grabbed the remote and turned up the volume without saying a word. I guess the decision had been made.

Ping ping beep beep beep…Ping ping beep beep beep

I was reminded just how much I hated the alarm on my cell phone. That robotic jingle that signals five-thirty in the morning had to be one of the top ten most annoying sounds in the world. Do you know what the number one most annoying sound is? It's when people say "I seen" instead of "I saw." Seriously. It's tied with fingernails on a chalkboard and loud chewing.

Ping ping beep—

I slapped my phone and crawled out of bed, then headed straight for the bathroom. Sitting on the toilet while scrolling through Facebook on my phone, I realized just how strange and kind of creepy our cultural habits had become. I was so tired that I contemplated going back to bed for a half hour, but I reminded myself that having thirty to forty minutes of quiet, alone time was worth the early wake-up.

Wearing old sweats and a t-shirt with my flamingo slippers, I stealthily crept downstairs and made a cup of coffee. I liked to sit at the table by the window, sip my coffee and read my devotional. This one was about God being a promise-keeper. His promises are true and He is faithful. I prayed and quoted Isaiah 41:10, making mental note to quote this verse to myself when I got scared or anxious about things.

With a few minutes left, I rummaged through the Murphy adoption file again. I still couldn't shake the feeling that I need to dig into this missing aunt. Maybe there was someplace I hadn't thought to check yet. I jotted down a few ideas to investigate and whispered an additional prayer for wisdom and direction.

"Maymay! You're up!" declared Tommy, coming down the stairs.

"I am! How about some breakfast?"

"No thanks."

"You really should eat something."

"Do I have to?"

I wondered what this kid's problem was with eating breakfast. I, for one, hardly ever turn down a chance to eat!

"Yes, Tommy. At least a little something. It'll be a long time 'til you get lunch at school. Want half a bagel with cream cheese?"

"How about chips and salsa?" He asked with eyes opened wide.

Let's see…chips are carbs and grains and the salsa is vegetables, so…why not? I got the kid chips and salsa and figured it was healthier than what a lot of kids eat first thing in the morning. Joseph and Carrie joined us, only they opted for the bagels. Days always start out smoother when I begin with my quiet time with God. But, I still needed to change that annoying alarm!

My desk at work was only wide enough to hold my computer, an open file and a legal size notebook where I take notes. My planner, other files and papers had to be stacked in a drawer to my right for quick access. Well, not quick, really…just close by.

"I've got two cases here that I could use your help with," Cole informed me, setting a fresh cup of Starbucks on my coaster.

"Pike Place or Veranda blonde?" I queried.

"Veranda with cream, of course."

"My favorite and the way I like it. You must really want my help."

Cole snickered. "You're the master at figuring out what forms are needed for what. These recent changes with the court have my head spinning."

"They're always changing things. And this is supposed to be a paperwork-reduction change! I'll walk you through it. Pull up a chair."

"I know I need to be on top of these things," Cole said with his head hanging and a defeated expression.

"You're putting in too many hours. There's no way you can keep up with this stuff when you're working twenty hours a day. You've gotta get some sleep, too. I really wish you'd quit the bouncer gig. You're starting to worry me."

Cole let a little smile slide onto his face. "At least someone worries about me."

I stopped typing and looked at my friend. Circles under his eyes, slumped over. He made me tired just looking at him.

"I tell ya what, I'll take care of these forms for you, but I want you to do me a favor."

"If it's quitting the bouncer gig—"

"No, no. I know you need the income, and I'd never try to demand something like that."

"Okay, then what's your favor?"

"Go with me to talk to Randy Turpin."

Cole exhaled sharply and leaned back in his chair. "Really? Why do you want to talk to this guy? He's not gonna tell you anything he hasn't told the police. And once you talk to him, he'll know who you are and that you're meddling in his wife's disappearance. This could be bad."

"Oh, come on! It won't be that big a deal. I just want to ask about his wife and see his face, how he responds. Maybe then I can shake this gnawing inside me that I need to dig deeper into her vanishing act. Please?"

"I'll think about it. But, you can go ahead and take care of those forms for me." Cole stood and gave me a wink as he pulled his chair back to his own desk.

"Well, you did bring me coffee."

"Yes, and your favorite, too!"

"You'll think about it…for real?"

Cole set his coffee down and looked me in the eye. "For real."

As I sat there working on page three of the fourth form Cole needed done, I began to regret letting him woo me with coffee.

"Charlotte, we've got a doozie," Mr. Baker exclaimed, practically running down the hall to my office. "This is gonna be a nasty custody case. Both sides are claiming abuse of the children."

He ruffled through some papers to find the one I needed to see.

"Who are we representing?" I asked.

"The husband," he replied, finally handing me the general information form.

"Ugh. This won't be fun."

"Does either side have proof?" Cole asked, leaning against my doorframe.

"Supposedly. He's supposed to bring in his proof tomorrow. I'd like you two to sit-in on the meeting."

"What time?" Cole asked.

Mr. Baker looked a little puzzled. "Eleven-thirty. Why? You need the day off or something?"

"No, no. Just Charlotte and I have an appointment in the morning."

"We do?" I shot Cole a confused look and he winked at me. "Uh, I mean, yeah, we do."

"Okay, just get here no later than eleven forty-five."

"Yes, Sir," Cole and I said in unison.

Mr. Baker nodded and walked back to his office. Once he was out of earshot, I waved Cole into my office.

"An appointment?" I asked.

"Yeah, to see Randy Tipton. I called and told him we just needed to finalize some things for Maddox's adoption. He reluctantly agreed. We meet at ten."

"You're the best."

"I know," he teased. "So, you have those forms done for me, yet?"

I gave him an incredulous look. "I take it back. You're a pain."

I threw a paper wad at him, but Cole just chuckled and walked away.

I had just begun to write out my questions for Randy Tipton when my cell phone rang. There in big letters on the screen was the name of Tommy's school. This always made my stomach churn because it was rarely about anything good.

"Hello?" I said with some trepidation.

"Ms. Ritter? I have Tommy here in my office. He's having some trouble today. He got very upset when one of his classmates started screaming. Tommy threw water on him and told him to 'chill out.'"

It was all I could do to not burst out laughing.

"Oh, dear," I struggled to speak without giggling. "Do you want me to talk to him?"

"Actually, we would prefer you come and get him."

I sighed. Now that he'd exhibited a problem behavior, they didn't want to deal with him. How many schools did we have to go through? These are supposed to be the professionals, and yet they called me at the smallest sign of trouble. So, he threw water on the kid in an attempt to cool him off. Did it work? I bet the teachers had wanted to try that at some point. I looked at the pile of work on my desk, and decided to just take it home.

"Alright. I'm on my way."

I informed Mr. Baker and Cole of the situation. Thankfully, because the Bakers had a nephew with autism, they were very empathetic to my struggles. Mrs. Baker had helped her sister with her son when schools kept sending him home for "behavior issues." Besides, I always got my work done one way or the other; so Mr. Baker never had a complaint.

On the way home, Tommy and I grabbed some cheap pizzas. Carrie had chopped peppers and onion, shredded cheese and bacon bits ready to toss on top and the oven preheated.

"Just long enough to toast the veggies and melt the extra cheese," I reminded her.

"I know. You go sit down. We can deal with this."

Now, I know most mothers would be suspicious of a child being this considerate, but not me. Well, not with Carrie. This was just how she was.

"Thanks, punkin. Put those brothers of yours to work, though. Don't do it all yourself."

We sat at the table, eating our franken-pizza as we jokingly called it. Tommy had to have some sour cream on his pieces. He was going through a sour cream phase. It was a little weird but harmless. I was flipping through papers in files. Joseph was watching a Film Riot video on his phone with headphones. Tommy was playing with empty soda cans, giving them voices and pretending they were his friends. Carrie was reading a seven-hundred-page book.

Once we were all done eating and dishes were in the dishwasher, I called the kids back to the table.

"Obviously, we each needed to retreat to our own corners, so to speak. But, surely we can spend a little time together before bed."

"How about a game?" Joseph asked. "It's been a while."

"Yes! Uno!" Carrie suggested.

"I'm cool with that," Joseph replied.

"I don't want to play a game," whined Tommy. "I need to take a bath."

I sniffed in his direction and concluded he was right.

"Okay, you can skip the game this time. Go bathe."

Tommy happily skipped away for a bath, and the rest of us played three rounds of Uno. I didn't win a single one. I think they cheated.

chapter five

The next morning, I met Cole at Indian River Coffee Company for a large, local cup o' joe. All this time I had been pressing to get this chance to speak with Randy Tipton, and now I was suddenly feeling uneasy about it. My face must have betrayed my thoughts.

"You getting cold feet?" Cole asked, taking a long sip of steaming hot Southern Pecan coffee.

"No…I mean, not really. Just getting jittery," I confessed.

"We don't have to do this."

"Yes. Yes, we do. I know it seems crazy, but this gut instinct of mine usually just kicks in when it's something involving my kids. And those instincts are always right. So, now it's telling me that this woman and her daughter need to be found. I can't ignore it."

Cole nodded. "Well, get you some of this coffee. It's really tasty… and maybe it'll bolster your confidence."

"Worth a shot, right?" I joked.

Getting our coffee to go, we hopped into my car and drove to the Tipton residence. It was in a rough part of

Palm Bay where the roads weren't maintained; neither were most of the houses. Except for the palm trees, one could easily assume they were in a backwoods area of Tennessee by all the chicken coops, trucks with rebel flags and even a few appliances on the front porches.

We arrived at the house and immediately spotted Randy Tipton sitting in a lawn chair, smoking a cigarette. He wore ripped jeans and a faded grey t-shirt, and sported a goatee and a neck tattoo that made him seem menacing. Cole patted my hand for reassurance and opened his car door. Time to get some answers.

"Mr. Tipton?" Cole asked in his deep, booming voice.

"Who wants to know?" Randy hollered back, still leaning back in his chair.

"The Baker Law Firm. We're handling the adoption of your nephew, Maddox. Ms. Charlotte, here, needs to ask you a few questions," Cole informed Randy while motioning in my direction. I stuck my hand in the air, confirming I was the lady with the questions.

"I've already answered all your questions and filled out all kinds of paperwork. What ya'll need now?"

Randy was clearly agitated. He tossed his cigarette on the ground and stomped on it.

"Well, Sir," I began, and then had to clear my throat. "There's a potential problem involving your wife."

"What kind of problem?" he snapped back, quickly standing.

"You see, she's biologically related to Maddox and as such, has rights to take over his guardianship. This could jeopardize the pending adoption. I really need to get in touch with her so she can sign the appropriate papers and we can move forward."

"If you're lookin' for Amber, then why are you here? She's missing! I'd have thought you'd know that."

"I am fully aware that she and your daughter, Lily, are both missing. I'm sure you're very upset about it—"

"Amber's nothin' but a trouble maker. I ain't exactly heartbroken she's gone," Randy admitted.

"Understood. But, Lily…she's only seven and your baby girl. That's gotta be tough."

Randy squinted at me; attempting to get a read on my angle.

"I'm a father myself," Cole added. "Can't imagine not having my little girl around."

"I get by," Randy muttered, pulling another cigarette from the pack and lighting it.

"We were hoping you might have some ideas as to where we could find Amber and Lily. It would help us with this adoption case, and could maybe lead to you seeing your little girl again."

We stood in awkward silence for a few moments. I had just about given up hope when Randy Turpin began to speak.

"Well, ya know…those druggies that Amber's sister hung around. The ones that ran that meth lab?"

"The lab that blew up, killing Maddox's parents?"

"Yeah, that one. Those druggies that were over there, they have other labs, too. And they're real violent types. Amber had caused some trouble with them. She kept trying to get her sister Autumn away from all that mess. I don't think it set well with them."

"So you're suggesting these druggies might know where Amber and Lily are? Maybe they did something to them?"

"It's possible," Randy said with a shrug.

"Did you tell this to the police?" Cole asked.

"I mentioned it."

"Know where we can find these people; these druggies?"

"Not really. Look at some of the vacant houses 'round here. Lots of meth labs are set up in foreclosed homes and there's plenty of those."

"Thanks," I replied, sarcastically.

Cole nodded towards the car. He thanked Randy for his time and we turned to leave. I glanced back over my shoulder to see Randy spit on the ground and pull out his cell phone to make a call.

"He's definitely shifty," Cole whispered. "Something's weird about him and his story."

"See!" I responded. "Even the sergeant I spoke with said Randy Tipton knew more than he was saying."

"Let's get back to the office. I have some ideas on how to locate the meth dealers."

"You think they're actually involved?" I asked as Cole opened the car door for me.

"I think it's worth investigating. I'll tell you my thoughts on the way to pick up my car…and maybe more coffee."

We hurried through the office door only to be greeted by the greatest of horrors. Okay, she's probably not the greatest horror, but I'm sure she's a close second. Our new paralegal, who was hired to ease Cole's work load, had become my nemesis of sorts. Ginny Wilson was thirty-five and a mother of seven year old twin boys; a tall blonde wearing a messy bun, high heels, a fancy manicure and always with a high-priced fancy coffee drink in her hand. She almost always seemed to casually mention how she didn't *need* to work because her husband was such a great provider. No, she worked as a paralegal in our firm because she "wanted to help children." Every time she started in with her rehearsed monologue, I imagined "In the Arms of an Angel" playing in the background. It was enough to make you nauseated.

Now, I know this makes me sound cynical and maybe even resentful, but hear me out. This woman has a way of grating on nerves that would make Job lose patience.

"You two are arriving late! We have a difficult case to prepare for!" she hissed.

"We've actually been working, thank you," Cole replied, rolling his eyes. "I started working on that case yesterday, by the way. You weren't here."

She glared at him, obviously annoyed. "I only work three days a week, Cole. You know, I don't need to be here. My work here isn't just a job. It's my passion."

I could see in Cole's face that he was ready to pounce on this subject by bringing-up (not for the first time) that she could always work pro bono. Since their last confrontation lasted an entire day, I decided to intervene.

"Cole, we need to go over some information before you start on that new case today, remember?"

Ginny butted-in. "What information?"

"Don't worry about it," I snapped. Then I more gently added, "You have enough on your plate with that new case. We'll be done in a bit, and Cole will be all yours."

I led Cole to my office with a sly grin on my face.

"What was that? 'All yours.' Thanks for handing me over to the enemy," Cole remarked.

I giggled. "You're welcome. Now, how do we find these drug dealers?"

"I put in a call to a buddy of mine that's a cop. If we can get some names from the meth lab explosion investigation, then we have a better chance of finding these people. We could even get descriptions if they have a record and were questioned or a person of interest. And if we can get that kind of information …"

"We can find them!"

Just as my fingers hit the computer keyboard, the phone rang. Cole answered.

"Baker Law." He listened for a second and then waved his hand in front of my face. Having my full attention, he silently mouthed "it's Randy" and began scribbling on a notepad he grabbed off my desk.

"Okay, thanks for the tip," Cole said, wide-eyed, before hanging up.

"More information?" I asked, grabbing the notepad from Cole's hands.

"He suddenly remembered that one of the guys that oversaw the meth lab had a noticeable tattoo."

"That's convenient," my sarcastic reply as I scanned Cole's notes. "Large gator head with open mouth on his left shoulder. Yeah, I'd say that's noticeable."

"Once my buddy calls me back, I'll ask him for drug-related convicts with gator tattoos. That should narrow our search."

"But doesn't this seem a bit…opportune?"

"It could be that Randy is sending us on a goose chase, sure. But, it could also be that he's mixed up with these people and couldn't just turn them in. Maybe he wants us to investigate because then we'd be the ones to find them and turn him in; not him."

"Interesting perspective," I admitted. "He just doesn't seem the type to be scared into silence. Still, you're right that it's worth digging a little deeper."

"Of course, we're just doing research here…no real investigating. That's for the police to do."

I gave Cole my pouty face and slumped my shoulders. "Fine."

He just rolled his eyes and took a gulp of coffee to bolster his defenses against Ginny and her inflated ego.

Having managed to finish those forms of Cole's I had promised to do, as well my own work on the new custody case, I left work to get home to the kids. Cole was still on the phone with his cop friend, but gave me a wink as I walked out the door. I hoped that meant he was getting good intel. My three cups of coffee were the maximum I would usually allow myself, but I pulled into the McDonald's drive-thru for one more pick-me-up. Ginny had whined all afternoon about her hyperactive twins and how her manicurist was out sick so she got stuck with someone new and therefore incompetent. That woman sucked the life out of me, and I needed energy to face the mountain of laundry that awaited me.

Joseph met me at the door with a hug and a weird grin.

"Hey, Mom, glad you're home!"

I was immediately suspicious. "Hey, buddy. What's up?"

"I…uh…kinda need your help."

"Okay," I set my bag and purse down on the kitchen counter and kicked my shoes off by the back door.

"I sort of forgot about a school project that's due."

I was right to be suspicious. "What project and when is it due?"

"Physics project. Due…tomorrow."

"What?"

"I know, I know. Please don't be upset."

"Joseph, you've got to keep up with assignments. Physics projects are typically easy to throw together at the last minute. What are you supposed to do?"

He stood in silence, obviously nervous about revealing the enormity of this project.

"Build a Rube Goldberg machine."

My jaw dropped and I just stared at my first born wondering how on earth he ever thought we could do this project in a single evening. I also wondered if we crawled on our knees and begged his teacher for mercy, if she'd give us a few more days. Doubtful.

"It's a machine that has multiple steps just to complete a simple task; kind of steampunk."

"I know what it is," I told him, insulted. Steampunk is something I've always found fascinating. "How many steps are you supposed to have for your machine?"

"Five."

"Good Lord. Do you have any ideas for this?"

"Yes! I have a sketch!" He pulled a sketchbook from his backpack and flipped to find the right page. "Here it is. We can use rope and some of our weights to open a drawer."

"This might actually be do-able. Let me change clothes and I'll meet you in the garage."

Sweat pants and baggy t-shirt donned, I entered the garage to see Joseph holding a wad of rope and staring forlorn into space.

"I'm really not sure how to do this," he muttered.

I glanced over his sketch again and started giving orders.

"Move that old dresser closer this way. We'll need the weight to move to pull the rope. How can we execute that?"

"Maybe it could roll down the weight bench? I mean, we could prop up the bench on one side like this…" Joseph set a crate under the end and let an eight-pound free weight roll down and onto the floor.

"That's a good start!" exclaimed Carrie, jumping in to help. "I read your assignment paper. You actually only need three steps but have to demonstrate five pysics principles. We can totally do this!"

I was ever grateful to have a science nerd in the family. With the three of us working together, we managed to come up with a system that released the weight to roll down the bench, pulling the rope that opened a drawer while also using the weight to crush an empty soda can in the recyling bin. Hey, for last minute, it wasn't too bad.

"Now, we have to video it," Joseph said.

"What? You didn't mention that part," I said, a bit aggravated.

"I'll use the iPad and email it to my teacher and then it's done. No big deal," Joseph assured me.

Carrie videoed him presenting his device which included a bit of theatrics on his part. He could be quite the showman when he wanted.

"Maymay, is there pesto?" Tommy called from the kitchen.

"Crap! Supper! How did I forget food?" I went running back into the house. "Yes, Tommy, there's pesto. Is that what you want?"

"Of course it is," he replied dryly.

Carrie helped me boil pasta and Joseph pulled a rotiserie chicken from the deli out of the fridge and began slicing. In a matter of minutes, we had a pretty tasty supper prepared.

"Today must be teamwork day," I told the kids when we sat down to eat.

"Why's that?" Joseph asked.

"Well, first, Cole and I worked together to get some information for a case. Then, we all worked to do your project. And just now we worked as a team to put together this meal."

"Go team!" Tommy yelled.

We all laughed.

"Go us!" added Carrie.

"We're number one!" Joseph cheered.

"Holy roosters!" hollered Tommy.

We have no idea where his favorite phrase come from, but sometimes—like this moment—it just seems perfectly apropos.

chapter six

Having managed to get everyone out the door on time, I actually arrived to work early. To my dismay, however, Ginny's car was parked and lights were on inside. This was supposed to be her day off, but I guessed she came in to work since Cole has spent time helping me with my side investigation. With a heavy sigh, a whispered prayer and a firm grip on my gas station coffee, I entered the office.

"Good morning, sleepyhead!" Ginny chirped.

"Uh, good morning. You're here early."

"Well, there's so much to do. Be a doll, and download some forms for me. Here's the list."

I held my breath and silently counted to five. "Ginny, I appreciate that you have a lot to do, but I have my own work to get done."

"But, you're our assistant," she stated with part confusion and part condescencion; still holding out that list.

"No. I'm the research assistant; meaning, I do research for information that assists Mr. Baker with his cases. And I have some serious amounts of research to get done. If you'll excuse me."

I began my walk down the hall towards my office once again whispering a prayer for Jesus to put His love in my heart and His hand over my mouth.

"It's just that I can't type so well with these new nails. I had them done again yesterday because my girl was finally back and she's the only one who does them right. You don't do anything with your nails so I figured you could just tap away on the computer and get these forms printed for me."

She was serious. Ya'll, she was completely serious. Ginny assumed I could I do this for her because I didn't get regular manicures. Not that I wouldn't love a good manicure, but not only could I not justify the expense, but I preferred to keep my nails short because of all the typing I do. Plus, on the ocassion that I need to restrain Tommy, nails that can scratch would be a really bad thing. But besides all that, Ginny wanted me to help her out to save her newly polished fingernails. Dear Lord.

"Ginny," I said turtly as I swung around in the hallway.

"Charlotte!" Cole yelled, swinging open the front door. "Come with me!"

I still had my purse, bag and coffee in my hands, but I just looked at Ginny and gave her a shrug before I followed behind Cole to his car.

"Where are we going?" I asked, struggling to keep pace with him.

"I'll tell you on the way."

We had barely shut the care doors when I began questioning Cole.

"Is this about the guy with the gator tattoo?"

"Yes. We have a possible location; a place to check out and see if he's there. I can ask him about Amber and Lily. You just stand there and use your spidey-senses."

"Funny. So, I'm not allowed to talk?"

"I'd rather you not. These aren't nice people, Charlotte. And this guy…get this, he has a kidnapping conviction."

"What? Seriously? So, he really could have taken them. But, he hasn't asked for ransom?"

"Maybe he has. Maybe Randy hasn't revealed that for some reason. I asked my buddy why the police haven't questioned him. He said they had no reason to because they didn't know about Amber trying to get her sister away from this guy and his drugs."

"What's this guy's name?"

Cole gave me a weird grin. "Gator."

"What's his *real* name?"

"That *is* his real name. No joke."

"His parents really named him Gator," I said incredulously, shaking my head. "Bless his heart."

It took about twenty-five minutes to get from the office down to Palm Bay to a location locals referred to as the Compound. It had been the start of a housing development with paved streets and designated lots for sale, but something went wrong along the way and whole area was abandoned. There were wooded areas throughout, and the streets winded through sometimes connecting, but sometimes coming to an abrupt end. It was a great location for many activities. Parents took their teenagers here to learn to drive. People came out to operate remote controlled cars and drones. Even Joseph had come out here with film club friends to film a zombie movie once. But, there was also a criminal element that liked the area for its conduciveness to hiding whatever it was you shouldn't be doing. The police had blocked the area off for a time after some apparent drag racing caused fatal accidents. But, they were far too busy to patrol such a large abanoned area all the time, and besides, there were plenty of ways to sneak in.

"We could never cover enough of this place to actually find someone; even if he does have a large gator tattoo," I complained to Cole.

"We don't have to go searching. My friend gave me directions to the usual hangout."

"Seriously?"

"He's done some undercover work, and has an informant out here. Supposedly, these guys aren't seriously dangerous. Mostly potheads."

"But, Gator has a kidnapping conviction. I'd say that makes him dangerous."

"We can always stop now, and just leave this alone," Cole said, seriously, stopping the car and looking me dead in the eye.

I took a deep breath to steady my nerves. "No. We can't stop. We need to find Amber and Lily, and this guy could be the key."

Traveling slowly over well-worn roads spotted with potholes and debris from palm trees, we came upon a dirt path leading into an area filled with tall grasses, saw palmettos and pine trees. Cole parked the car and the two of us hesitantly exited the sanctuary of his '01 Ford Explorer and walked to the edge of the trail.

"Stay behind me," Cole instructed. He didn't have to tell me twice.

I was sweating under the bright heat of the sun, but ominous, dark clouds had gathered nearby. Somehow the threat of a thunderstorm felt appropriate for the moment. A few yards down this path into the Florida version of "the woods," we heard voices. Men were talking. I was thankful that the tone of the conversation sounded friendly and not like an argument. Cole reached behind him and held his hand in front of me, silently mouthing "stop."

"Hey, fellas," Cole hollered. "I'm here to see Gator. Is he here?"

I couldn't see around Cole's broad shoulders. Peeking around his outstretched arm, I caught a glimpse of three men standing near a clearing not far from us.

"I'm Gator," one of the men yelled back. "Who're you?" he asked, sounding very much like a, uh…well, a redneck.

"My name is Cole. A friend of mine told me I could find you here. Got a minute?"

After a little whispering with his buddies, Gator walked forward. He wore a t-shirt emblazoned with a beer advertisement and a scantily clad woman; the sleeves cut off to reveal the gator head tattoo on his upper arm. He dropped a cigarette from his hand as he strolled up to us. His face weathered like someone who worked outdoors displayed a crooked smile that made you think he was up to something.

"The only friend of mine who would give a stranger directions out here is a cop," he said quietly. "I'm assuming you're a cop, too?"

"No, no. We actually work for a law firm. We're looking into a case…well, it's kind of a long story," Cole tried to explain.

"Do you know Amber Tipton?" I asked, boldly stepping out from behind Cole.

"Amber? Isn't she Autumn's sister?" This guy was sounding way too friendly and relaxed. It was weirding me out.

"Yes, she was…is. She's missing. And we heard she gave you trouble when she was trying to get Autumn away from your—"

"Business!" Cole interrupted. "We were told she meddled in your business."

Cole gave me a look when he said that. I caught on that we should keep the conversation generic, and not mention drugs.

"Look, if you're talkin' 'bout the meth situation, I don't really do that stuff. I mean, I was there a couple times meetin' my supplier. Weed, man. That's all I do."

"And apparently kidnapping," I spoke boldly again. But as soon at the words left my mouth, I felt a twinge in my stomach.

"So, you've done some digging," Gator remarked. "How much do you know?"

This question made me feel really nervous. Cole cleared his throat and prepared to answer, but Gator jumped in again.

"Okay, so yes I technically kidnapped my son," Gator began. "But, and that's a big but...he's my son and his mother was all whacked-out on heroine. I had to get him outta there."

"Wait...what? You took your son away from his mother while she was strung out on heroine? You were charged and convicted of kidnapping," Cole reminded him.

"I know. I was on probation for possession of marijuana, and my baby momma's parents don't like me much. They fought to get me behind bars. They got custody of my boy, now."

Gator's face turned sullen. I actually felt sorry for him.

"So, then I guess you don't know where we could find Amber," Cole said with a sigh.

"You said she's missing?" asked Gator. "What about that no-good husband of hers? There's a piece of work for ya. That dude's got anger issues. Autumn told me he beat her sister, and she was trying to get away."

"Makes sense," I said to Cole. "We found that restraining order."

"Guess we're back where we started," Cole lamented.

We thanked Gator for his time, and practically ran back to the car to get out of there. Last thing we needed was to get caught up in a drug bust or something.

"Apparently, Gator is your friend's informant. He said his friend was a cop," I said to Cole as we drove out of the Compound.

"I guess so. And he definitely doesn't come across as someone who would kidnap a woman and a little girl."

"So, now what?" I asked, feeling defeated.

Cole smiled. "Now, we get coffee."

I spent the rest of my day at the office, working on the upcoming custody dispute case and ignoring all things related to Amber and Lily Tipton. Meeting Gator was just a waste of time and nothing but a dead end.

"I'm leaving now," Ginny informed me, poking her head into my office.

"See you in a couple days," I said, trying to smile and be polite.

"Oh, I'll be back tomorrow." She apparently took my politeness as an invitation to come in and chat.

"We've got a good handle on this, Ginny. You don't need to work extra days."

"Well, I'd rather be here and get stuff done just in case you and Cole go on one of your excursions again," she remarked, smiling and giving me a wink.

"Excursion? We had to meet with someone. That's all."

"You came back with coffee, all chatty with each other. But, whatever. None of my business."

"Agreed. Have a nice night," I hinted, smiling and waving. She took the hint.

I finished jotting down reminders on my desk calendar and stuffed my planner into my bag alongside my stash of Lucky's trail mix and my phone. Mr. Baker waved from his desk as I left the office. It took a minute to get my bag, coffee mug and myself situated in the van. Finally, on the road heading for home, I weighed the tough decision of taking either Wickham Road or interstate 95. These days, it's six of one, half a dozen of the other as to the possibility of sitting in a traffic jam. I opted for the interstate, and whispered a prayer.

A few minutes into my trip home, the gas light came on.

"Seriously?" I said aloud to no one but myself, and I flipped on my blinker just before the next exit.

As I drove onto the exit ramp, I realized the car behind me was coming up quick. Before I could speed up, the other car came along side me causing me to swerve onto the shoulder. Instead of going ahead of me, though, the car stayed to close to my left. I couldn't see inside because the windows were so tinted. Panicked, I tried to slow down to let them pass but finally had to slam the brakes. My van skid and a cloud of dust rose into the air as I narrowly missed a roadside sign. The other car stopped and began to back up...until the sirens were heard. Coming up right behind us was a sheriff's car. I stayed on the shoulder and let him go after that crazy driver, but he pulled behind me!

"Ma'am, are you alright?" he asked through my open window.

"Yes, officer. I take it you saw that person trying to run me off the road?"

"Sure did. I radioed his tag number and direction of travel. We'll have someone caught up to him in no time.

There's a speed trap just down the road where he was headed. You sure you're okay?"

"I'm sure. Thank you." I suddenly realized I had been holding my breath. I inhaled deeply and tried to calm myself.

"He wasn't just trying to get by. He wanted you to wreck or stop. We have seen some incidents where criminals will do this and then rob the person. Sometimes there's assault or even rape involved. No way to know how or why they targeted you…unless you have a suspicion?"

"No, Sir," I lied. I hate to have to admit that, but it's true. I lied. I did have a suspicion. But, I couldn't exactly go into all that. I silently repented for my transgression.

"It might help if you filed a report. You can do it tomorrow if you like. Here," he handed me a card with his name and badge number and the address of the sheriff's office.

"Thank you. I'll do that."

Pumping gas was an ordeal. I was constantly looking around nervously, and the slam of a car door made me jump. By the time I got home, my hands were shaking; I barely got the back door unlocked.

"Mom, are you okay?" Carrie asked, worried.

"I'm fine. Just almost had an accident and it shook me up a little. Ya know, I really don't feel like cooking. Suggestions?"

"Pizza!" yelled Tommy from the living room, with his headphones still on.

"Let's go out somewhere. We've got some coupons," said Carrie, looking through the coupon drawer in the kitchen. "How about Burger King?"

"Yes!" Tommy squealed, excited. "My favorite!"

I put on a brave face, drove the kids two minutes down the road and went through the drive-thru. As soon as were safely back in the house, I locked the doors and checked the windows. We ate supper and chatted, and I managed to keep the conversation funny and light-hearted. Later, once the kids were in bed, it took a cup of sleepy-time tea and four episodes of Star Trek Enterprise on Netflix to get me to sleep.

chapter seven

Wake up. Look at time on phone. Groan. Toss and turn. Dose off. Repeat. That was how my night went. At six-thirty, I called Mr. Baker and told him how horrible I felt, but that I'd work from home for the day. He was fine with that.

"I know Ginny gets on your nerves. Truthfully, I would have let her go already, but she does decent work and doesn't mind the few hours as we need her."

"I know she helps especially when we have a lot to get done in a short amount of time. It's just with my lack of sleep and this headache…"

"No worries. Janet says to let her know if you need anything. She'll be out towards your part of town for a library event."

"I appreciate that. Thank you. I promise to let her know if I think of something."

It was difficult not to ask for Janet for some of her homemade gumbo. Good food always lifted my spirits, and that gumbo was seriously good.

Of course the kids wanted to stay home to "help" since I didn't feel well. I convinced them I'd be fine and got them all to school on time. On the way home, Cole called. Don't worry. I answered while sitting in the McDonald's drive-thru waiting for coffee, and put him on speaker phone while I drove.

"Sorry you're feeling bad," Cole said sweetly. "You're not upset about the dead end with Gator, are you?"

"Well, it's kind of related to all that, I think. I need your opinion. You should know what happened after work yesterday."

I filled him in on the whole scary scenario in between sips of coffee.

"Are you sure you're alright? No wonder you're all a wreck today!"

"I'm not 'all a wreck.' Just tired. Who would do this to me, though? Could it just be coincidence?"

"No way. It's Gator, or one of his buddies. I guarantee it. He played all nice and easy going, but he wanted to scare you into leaving things alone."

"You really think so?"

"I do. You need to be careful. Go file that police report. You should have something to protect yourself."

"I have pepper spray."

"Somebody's gotta get awfully close for that to work."

"I'll sign-up for a karate class," I joked.

"I'm serious. But, first things first. Go to the sheriff's office."

I called the number on the card the deputy had given me and verified that I should come in and file some type of report. Feeling a teensy bit energized from the coffee, I went to the sheriff's office and filled out some paperwork. Sheriff Ivey, here in Brevard County, is a much-loved and well-respected man. While I was waiting to have someone look over my report, I noticed a brochure. In it, the sheriff himself was quoted; encouraging citizens of our county to arm themselves.

"The best law enforcement agencies in the country have a response time in minutes," Sheriff Ivey states. The brochure goes on to suggest that an armed criminal can take your life in a matter of seconds. Maybe Cole's suggestion was something worth considering.

It was our mid-week service at Greater Life Worship Center. I always enjoyed Bible study. Ours was relaxed, casual, and served coffee. We arrived early (miracles never cease!), and the Gaggle of Grannies cornered me first thing.

"You look peak-ed," commented Mammaw Sellers. "You're not eating right."

"You look tired," added Little Momma. "You feelin' sick?"

"No, ma'am. I just didn't sleep well," I confessed.

"She almost had an accident," Carrie blabbed. I gave her an annoyed look and she took Tommy down the hall to his class. Joseph went off to find his friends.

"An accident? What happened?" asked Granny.

"Some idiot tried to run me off the road. The sheriff's deputy said a group of criminals are causing people to either crash or stop in an uninhabited area so they can rob them."

All the grannies gasped and began talking at once about "what the world has come to" and "the last days." Not that I disagreed, but I couldn't get a word in edgewise.

"You need something to protect yourself," Momma Pat told me.

"Listen to her," said Granny (Momma Pat's mother). "They call her Granny Oakley down at the firing range."

I burst out laughing, but the grannies just looked at me…dead serious.

"I have my concealed carry permit. You should, too," Momma Pat informed me.

"Are you…packing?" I asked.

"Always! You need to get educated on guns and self-defense and licenses. This is where you should go." She handed me a card for Femme Fatale Arms and Training.

"They're not too far from the house. I'll check it out."

"If you start to chicken out, call me. I'll go with you," Momma Pat offered, giving me one of her world's best hugs.

"Promise," I committed.

After the weekly Bible study (which was about the whole armor of God, oddly enough), I drove us home. We talked and laughed the entire way. It wasn't until we walked in the back door that fear gripped me. What if we had been followed? What if someone was here at the house?

"Freeze!" I yelled to the kids, and they actually froze in place.

"Mom, what's wrong?" Joseph asked, a bit shocked at my outburst.

"Stay with me and we're gonna walk through the house together."

"Is something going on? This is weird," Carrie added.

"Just walk with me."

We went room to room together, and I prayed out loud, thanking God for being our Protector, our Refuge in a time of trouble. The kids basically just looked at me as if I had three heads and spoke Klingon. When it was obvious that everything was fine, I let them go their own way. Of course, none of them wanted to be separate from the group.

"Hey, Joseph, let's watch an episode of Malcolm in the Middle before bed," Carrie suggested.

"Yeah, why not," he replied.

"I'll watch, too," Tommy said, to our surprise. Then he grabbed his iPad and headphones and sat next to them on the couch.

Cole had taken the liberty of informing Mr. Baker about my interstate incident. He agreed with Cole that I needed to be cautious and think about protecting myself and the kids. So, when I asked to take extra time at lunch to check out this women's gun and training place, my boss was happy to oblige.

Walking into Femme Fatale Arms, I wasn't really sure what to expect. In the front, they had a display of beautiful leather purses that had special concealed compartments for your weapon. There were t-shirts, holsters, and even jewelry. I pretty much made a straight line for the glass cases filled with guns.

"Hello, welcome to the store. Is there something I can help you find?" Asked the woman behind the counter.

"I'm not sure. I'm looking for something for protection, but I have a lot of questions…a lot of concerns."

"Alright. Let's get started. What do you want to know?"

"Well, first off, let me tell you that I'm not even sure I'm going to buy a gun."

"Not a problem. We are here to educate women about weapons, about options, about protecting themselves. I'm Marcy, by the way."

"Nice to meet you."

"What's your biggest concern?" she asked kindly.

"Safety. I have kids at home, and one of them is autistic. I can't have the gun easily accessible, but at the same time, it needs to be…accessible."

"Understood. I always recommend a good gun safe, and we have one here that is biometric."

"That sounds like something from Star Trek."

Marcy laughed. "It's pretty cool. It scans your fingerprint; so you're not fumbling with keys in an intense emergency situation. And it holds over thirty prints so you can input all your fingers in case maybe one hand is injured."

"I like this. Safe but accessible. Okay that's one concern figured out. Now, if I were to get a gun, the problem is I'm obviously a bit petite and I don't have strong hands."

"Not an issue," she assured me.

Marcy, deciding it best to start with absolute basics, began by showing me ammo, and how different bullets have different results.

"A lot of stores will direct women to a .22, but all that's really good for is shooting squirrels and paper."

"Obviously, I don't see either of those as threats," I quipped.

"Exactly. I recommend a nine millimeter like this Sig Sauer over here."

She took out a rather large gun, removed the magazine and handed demonstrated how to slide it back, pull the trigger and such. Then she handed it to me. Nervously, I took hold of the gun, used my left hand to slide it back like she had shown me, and pointed it toward a rather large wall safe to pull the trigger. It was much easier than I had anticipated.

"Now, if it were loaded there would obviously be a little kickback, but nothing you couldn't handle," she informed me.

We spent the next half hour with her showing me guns, asking which ones I liked, which ones felt secure in my hand, and which ones were easiest for me to handle. She told me about the classes they offer for everything from getting your concealed carry license to cleaning your gun and tactical shooting. I ended up really liking one of the biggest guns she had shown me, but I wasn't ready to take that step…not just yet.

Marcy was very kind, extremely informative, and never pressured me. Leaving there, I felt like I had made some real progress towards a big decision. I had been so focused on what I wanted to ask when I got inside the gun shop that I hadn't paid attention to where I parked. Having to stand on the sidewalk and scan the parking lot for my van ultimately had a profitable outcome. It occurred to me that Gator couldn't possibly have been the one to come after me on I-95. We had taken Cole's car. The only questionable character that knew what my van looked like and exactly where I worked was Randy Tipton.

When I arrived at the office, Ginny was standing in the hallway giving Cole flack about something.

"Cole, come to my office," I sort-of demanded.

"He's busy," snapped Ginny. "We are up to our eyebrows in paperwork."

"You don't even have eyebrows, Ginny. You draw yours on!" I snapped back.

She stood there in shock while Cole tiptoed away and into my office ahead of me. I just gave Ginny a shrug and walked away.

"What was that?" Cole questioned once I had closed my office door behind me.

"She gets on my nerves, and they're already a bit frayed. I'll apologize later."

Cole chuckled. "I didn't say you needed to apologize. She's been impossible all morning. How'd your lunch break visit to the gun shop go?"

"Very well! I learned so much, but that story will have to wait. I realized something while I was looking for my van. We need to dig deeper into Randy Tipton's files."

Once I had Cole filled-in on my sidewalk revelation, he agreed to help me go back through Randy's file to see if we missed anything. He even offered to call the Home Improvement store where Randy worked and speak to his manager.

"But, first I'd better get some things done on this custody battle case that's come in. Ginny was right. We have tons of work to do," Cole admitted.

"Sure. Of course. And I guess I'd better go apologize," I whined.

My attempt to tell Ginny how sorry I was for my verbal attack fell flat. She muttered something about it not being a big deal and stomped off to make copies. I was going to have to pray about this and get some help from the Big Guy. Dealing with difficult people was not one of my talents.

Just before the work day ended, Cole knocked on my office door.

"I spoke with a co-worker of Randy's," Cole began. "He said that he remembered when Amber and Lily first disappeared because Randy was really torn up about it. Said the guy was emotional and distracted for a few days. Then finally Randy went to his manager and asked for some time off. He said Randy even bought one of those build-it-yourself sheds from the store to work on while he was off work. Probably to keep his mind occupied."

"A shed?" I asked.

"Yeah. You know, like to store tools or a mower or whatever."

"I know what a shed is, Cole. But, Randy didn't have one."

"How do you know that?"

"I know that because we were at his house and the entire yard was in clear view. I could even see the back yard when we were on the next street over, leaving his subdivision."

"You were paying attention to all that?"

"Of course I was! Trust me. No shed."

"Well, that's interesting."

"Isn't it though? And if he's so distraught and can't focus, why attempt building his own shed? He could have gotten one pre-assembled."

"I didn't think about that," said Cole with one raised eyebrow.

I grinned.

"What?" Cole questioned. "Why are you smiling like that?"

"It's just kind of funny how much you look like the Rock when you do that eyebrow thing."

Cole rolled his eyes. "You're just using flattery so I won't feel so stupid for not catching-on to all this about Randy. You're quite the detective, Charlie."

"You know, you're the only person I let call me that. My name is Charlotte."

Cole gave me a wink and started for the door. "Yeah, whatever. You like it."

chapter eight

Get home safely…check. Kids' homework…check. Supper (actually cooked at home)…check. Quality family time…nope. Everyone retreated to their rooms. Sometimes we used all our social energy at school and work, and there was nothing left for home. It used to bug me, but I learned to accept this as a family quirk. We simply have days when we just need to be alone, and that's okay.

With a cup of hot tea in hand and fuzzy socks on my feet, I sat up in bed with my laptop ready to work. If Randy Tipton built a shed, where did he have it and why? It wasn't on his property…or was it?

Bringing up the Brevard county property appraiser website, I began searching for property in Randy's name. Nothing showed up other than the house we visited. A thought popped into my head and I searched under Amber's maiden name. Sure enough, a ten-acre "unimproved" lot showed up on the screen. This acreage even had a sizeable pond fed by an artesian well. Low visibility, water access… the perfect hiding place.

I texted Cole, and he responded with *"call the police."* He had a way of taking the wind out of my sails. I didn't want to call the police. Chances were good they'd never get permission to check out the property. What would they say when they requested a warrant…a lawyer's research assistant told us she had a hunch?

Next, I texted Su. She was my source of wisdom when I had a decision to make. But, she didn't immediately respond. Knowing she had three kids on the autism spectrum and went to school full time, I didn't feel jilted. She'd text back when she could find the time. I thought about what she would tell me, and realized her first bit of advice would be to pray about it. That should have been obvious to me, but it's easy to get so wrapped up in a situation that you reverse the order of remedies and save the best for last. So, I prayed. Asking for wisdom, direction and safety, I left it in God's hands and set my work aside. Clicking on Netflix, I figured just one episode of The Great British Baking Show, and I'd go to sleep.

Saturday finally arrived. Joseph went to work on a film project with his friends. Carrie had a softball sleepover the night before, and would be taken to the game that afternoon by her coaches. I arranged for Tommy to spend the day with a family friend, Ms. Cathy. She had been his teacher when he was younger, and she loved to babysit him from time to time. They had a special bond. She also knew how much I appreciated the break.

Today was all about work, though. I was going to go snooping…er…do some observation in north Brevard. Cole texted and asked if I had called the police. When I replied that I hadn't, he called.

"And why not?" he demanded, the second I answered his call.

"They won't be able to do anything with that information. It's not enough. I'm gonna drive out there—"

"You're gonna what?"

"Drive out there and look around a little. No big deal."

"Why on earth would you do something stupid like that?"

"I just need to see if there's anything suspicious out there. Then I could give the police more information; maybe something actionable!"

"You don't know who or what is out there. You have nothing to protect yourself. This is a really bad idea. Don't go."

"But, Cole, what about Amber and Lily? Someone has to be looking into this; doing some searching. What if I find them?"

"What if you find bodies?"

His words froze me. I hadn't allowed myself to consider that possibility.

"Charlotte?"

"I'm here," I sighed.

"Just wait a few minutes. I'll go with you."

Cole drove his old beater truck, an eighties GMC that looked as though it had been driven in a demolition derby. He figured it could handle rough, dirt roads and any debris we come across while out in "the boonies." Plus, the two persons of interest in our amateur investigation had seen my van and Cole's Explorer. This truck would give us an element of surprise. At least, that was the idea.

"You know, I'm an only child. But, I always wanted a big brother," I confessed to Cole as he drove us toward Randy's property.

"I have a big brother. They're not that great," Cole joked.

"I happen to know that you adore your big brother."

"Yeah, well."

We rode in silence that last few miles, and then I helped to navigate while studying the map on my phone's GPS.

"This is it. Maybe there's a road or a path along here somewhere."

The truck bumped along the pitted dirt road. For miles around, all we could see was overgrown land filled with palms and pines; osprey and blackbirds flying overhead, an occasional tortoise crawling along the roadside. A few minutes down the road, I noticed a small road of sorts. It was barely wide enough for the truck, but we turned onto it anyway. Branches brushed against the windows and the bumps were more plentiful. Cole had to slow to a snail's pace to save his wheel alignment and to keep me from getting motion sickness.

The trees began to clear and we found ourselves driving into a grassy clearing. Just a few feet ahead of us was a rather large body of water; large enough that it contained a decent sized island with plenty of space to build a house or a shed.

"I though you said he had a pond on this property. This is a lake!" exclaimed Cole.

"What's the difference exactly? I've always wondered."

"Doesn't matter now. We're here and we don't have a boat. Hand me those binoculars."

Cole took the binoculars and carefully stepped out of the truck. I followed after him and we walked to the edge of the water. He put the binoculars to his eyes and made adjustments, pointing them towards the island.

"There's acres of un-cleared land here," I told him. "If Lily and Amber are here, they could be anywhere."

"They're on that island," said Cole, matter-of-factly.

"What makes you say that?"

"Because there's the shed."

Cole pointed and handed me the binoculars. There, practically hidden by a grouping of trees, was a wood shed. Its lone window covered by a plywood board.

"Now, we call the police," Cole stated.

"Yeah. Call the police."

We decided I should call Sergeant Atwood since he had given me the lead on Randy Tipton.

"There's several problems here," he told me, sounding agitated. "One, you have no business being there. Two, you could be in danger. And three, you're out of my jurisdiction. Lucky for you, I have a friend in the sheriff's office that I'm going to send your way. I'm going to tell this friend that you were wandering around and got lost. He'll have your location, and if *he* has any suspicions, given what he knows about this Tipton guy; he can look into it. You two will leave as soon as he finds you. Understood?"

"Yes, Sir," I squeaked nervously. "Understood."

"Someone's on the way?" Cole asked.

"Yes, but it'll be a while. And the sergeant didn't seem inclined to investigate. Mostly he wants to make sure we leave."

"I have an idea, but for the life of me I don't know why I'm even suggesting this."

"What? What's your idea?" I begged.

Cole rolled up his pant legs and then searched for a long tree branch. When he found one the length he was looking for, he waded a few feet into the water and stuck the branch down to the bottom.

"Just as I thought," he said. "This is pretty shallow. We might be able to wade across."

"You know, the Indian River Lagoon is only four feet deep. You can wade from one side to the other," I informed him.

"Thank you for that bit of Florida trivia," Cole quipped. He kept wading and was nearly to the other side when he waved me over to join him.

"You want me to cross, too?" I questioned.

"That's the idea. Do you want to investigate or not?"

I rolled up the legs on my nicest jeans and shuffled my way to Cole. The water was cold and murky. Twice something brushed against my leg and gave me the heebie jeebies.

Stepping onto the island, we heard a noise coming from the shed. Cole motioned for me to follow him and we stepped quickly through some brush to the side of the small wooden structure. The one tiny window had a piece of plywood nailed over it so that we couldn't see inside. I walked slowly toward the door and saw that it was chained and locked. More noises from inside startled me. Cole stepped up behind me and examined the shed.

"Something's inside, no doubt," I whispered to him.

More noises; only this time we could tell it was a voice. Someone was inside that locked shed.

"She's talking. See, I told you he had her in there," I whispered enthusiastically.

"We don't know if it's her or not. And we have no way of opening that door."

"So what should we do?"

Before Cole could answer me, we heard a car bouncing its way down the dirty road. Not knowing if it was the sheriff's deputy or Randy Tipton coming to check on his hostages, Cole and I ducked into a patch of tall grass along the waterline and remained silent and still.

The car stopped and a door opened. I struggled to see through the grass and yet keep myself hidden.

"I see your car, but I don't see you. This is Deputy Crowder," the man called out.

Cole stood and grabbed my hand, pulling me behind him through that nasty, cold water.

"What are you two doing out there?" the deputy asked.

"We heard a person's voice from inside that shed," I said, pointing to the island behind me.

"A person?"

"Yes, Sir. We believe there's a woman inside," Cole said.

"Actually, a woman and her young daughter," I added.

"Wait here," said the deputy and he waded the water while asking if anyone was there and needed help.

"I'll ask again; is anyone in there? Does anyone need assistance?" Deputy Crowder yelled at the shed. No answer.

We waited for five or six minutes and not a sound was heard. The deputy crossed the water again, and was none too happy with us.

"I think you two need to quit investigating private property. Can you find your way back out to the main road or do you need assistance?"

We assured him we could find our way and drug our soaking wet selves to the truck. Cole and I rode in silence for what seemed like a long time.

"You're going to have to let this one go, Charlie," he finally said.

Sighing heavily, I nodded in agreement.

"You did your best. You've pointed the police in the right direction. All you can do now is let them take over and see what happens. Maybe they'll get a warrant and open that shed. That's a possibility."

"I know."

Cole, sensing my despair, decided to be a comedian. "I've heard stories about having to bail bratty little sisters out of trouble. Now I know."

I patted his shoulder. "Funny. Very funny."

Sunday morning arrived, and I was grateful to have managed to sleep until eight before Tommy knocked on my door.

"Maymay, are you awake?" he asked.

"Technically, yes," I replied, sarcastically.

"Do we have chips and salsa?"

I shook my head in disbelief. Who on earth wants chips and salsa for breakfast? Tommy, that's who. I opened my door and he had to step back to let me out of the room. Then, he followed me to the kitchen as I pulled the chips from the pantry and a jar of salsa from the fridge.

"Help yourself," I told him. He did.

Starting the Keurig, I leaned against the kitchen counter and purposely took a few deep breaths. Part of me wanted to just stay in pajamas and lounge around the house.

"Hey, Mom!" Carrie greeted me. "Want me to make us all some kolaches?"

"Sure! There should be a couple cans of biscuits in the fridge, and the Little Smokies sausages are in the fridge in the garage."

"Do we have enough cheese?"

"We should, but you'd better check before you get started."

Carrie found half a bag of shredded cheddar and went to work making breakfast. The black, magical device dispensed my coffee. I inhaled the amazing aroma of the Toasted Coconut coffee and took a long, glorious drink. I suddenly felt awake enough to pick out something to wear to church.

"Good morning," mumbled Joseph, shuffling into the kitchen with barely opened eyes and serious bed head.

"My coffee just finished. I'll start yours," I told him. "Toasted Coconut or hazelnut?"

"Either. Both."

"One of those mornings, huh? Me, too."

Before I knew it, Carrie had the kolaches in the oven. My mother and grandmother would have called them pigs in a blanket, but when we briefly lived in Texas, we picked up the term kolaches. As Florida residents, few people ever knew what we were talking about; but when they tasted them…well, who cared what they were called?

Once the coffee kicked in some more and I tried on three different dresses, it was smooth sailing getting everyone ready and out the door for church. Tommy knew right where his shoes were and everything. We arrived just early enough for Carrie to take Tommy to his class before she met Joseph and the rest of the youth group for their own version of Sunday school. The downside was that they left me standing in the foyer alone and the gaggle of grannies came at me full force.

"Oh, I'm so glad you're here early," exclaimed Momma Pat.

"Honey, we've got to talk," added Little Momma.

"Nothing bad, though. Don't worry," Mammaw Sellers explained.

Granny spoke-up, "Now, now. Settle down, ya'll. We've only got a minute before church starts."

"So, what's going on?" I asked. "There's something I need to know?"

"There's some*one* you need to know," Little Momma said, giggling.

"Oh, no. Not another setup," I complained.

"But, you haven't heard about this one yet! He's a fine lookin' man and he's new to this area," Momma Pat informed me.

"He's a widower and his two children are in college," Mammaw Sellers stated.

"So good lookin'," Little Momma added.

"Woah, ya'll. I appreciate the fact that you spotted this eligible bachelor and apparently learned his entire life history. But, I'm not looking to date anyone right now. Besides, what would I do? Go up to this man and say, 'hey, my adoptive grannies said you're fine and single. Wanna go out?'"

"Sure!" exclaimed Little Momma. "Try that! Might work."

The others giggled and I just rolled my eyes and smiled. It took us a minute to all hug each other before we went to our seats. I left the gaggle with a package of pocket tissues, a handful of individually wrapped peppermints, and a business card from the new man in town.

Pastor Smith delivered a terrific sermon about helping those who can't themselves. Unfortunately, this brought back that nagging sensation I'd had to uncover what happened to Amber and Lily Tipton. Our excursion to the shed did nothing but convince the cops we were some kind of crazy. Someone needed to find Amber and her daughter, and I felt even more convinced that I was the one to do it. While still in the church parking lot, I sent a group text to the Grannies that I had an unspoken prayer request regarding a case at work. I gave them that little bit of specificity so they wouldn't think I was praying about the good-lookin' widower.

That evening, the kids had opted to watch one of the Star Wars movies together while I tidied up the house. One of the things on my to-do list was to set the trash cans out by the road for pick-up the next morning. Usually, Joseph would handle this, but he had aced his English exam so I gave him a night off from chores.

It was already dark outside so I grabbed a little flashlight from the junk drawer in the kitchen. The lights by the back door had a mind of their own. Sometimes the motion sensor would detect the tiniest lizard and flip on the lights. Other times, you could do jumping jacks in front of the thing and still be left in the dark. This was one of those times. The lights refused to turn on. But, the street light by the neighbor's house illuminated the curb enough I felt confident I could roll the trash out there without incident.

I grabbed the first can and began to pull, but as I took a step backwards, I bumped into something. But then that something grabbed me, an arm around my chest and a hand securely over my mouth.

"You've gotten nosy and it's gonna cost you," the man growled.

My heart was beating so fast I could feel it throbbing in my ears. I broke out in a cold sweat, and I struggled to get a good breath through my nose.

"Stay away from the compound. Leave all this alone or you'll regret it," he whispered ominously while tightening his grip.

Suddenly, Tommy swung open the kitchen door and the lights came on, illuminating the entire side of the house. The stranger released me and took off running. He was dressed in all dark clothes so I couldn't tell anything about him. He ran until he was out of sight. I never saw a car or bike or anything.

"Who was that?" Tommy asked excitedly.

"No one, buddy. No one at all. Go back inside, okay?"

He did as he was told. I grabbed the trash can, threw open the lid and puked inside. After a few minutes of sobbing, my head in an outdoor trash can, I finally calmed down enough to roll the trash to the curb.

For some reason, I opted to keep silent about the ordeal. I didn't tell the kids or the Grannies. I didn't even text Cole. After a long shower, and a thorough check of all the windows and doors, I crawled into bed. Hours passed before I fell asleep, and images of a man in black haunted my dreams.

It was around six Monday morning that I finally texted Cole. He called me right away, and I gave him all the details of the night before.

"You need to file a report with the police," he instructed.

"And tell them what? A stranger warned me to stay away from the compound? That's hardly a crime."

"He threatened you!"

"It was pretty vague."

"Why aren't you taking this seriously?" Cole asked, frustrated.

"I am. Believe me, I'm shaken. But, I'm also realistic. The police would have nothing to go on. There's no point."

Cole sighed. "This guy...he mentioned the compound? It's probably Gator."

"Didn't sound like him. I've never bought that Gator was our guy."

"Then why mention that specific place? Why not mention the shed?"

"Randy Tipton wouldn't mention the shed. He'd try to send us chasing after Gator again."

"Good point," Cole admitted.

My phone began to beep with another call coming in. I let it go to voicemail.

"Maybe you should take today off and rest. You sound worn out. Want me to bring you anything?"

"No, thanks. I'm coming in to work. Sitting at home just makes me feel worse."

I hung up with Cole, and played the voicemail message.

"Ms. Ritter, this is Sergeant Atwood with the Palm Bay Police Department. I was notified by the sheriff's office that they picked up the man suspected of being the one who ran you off the road the other day. Interesting thing is, his name is Roy Tipton and his brother is Randy. I'm thinking you should stay clear of Randy while this is investigated. I informed the sheriff deputy of your situation with Randy's missing wife and all that. If you have any questions, give me a call."

With shaking hands, I set my phone down on my bathroom counter. Chills ran down the back of my neck. What had I gotten myself into? This guy was obviously upset that I gotten nosy, and he was willing to harm me to get me to go away. I texted Su asking for prayer, and messaged Momma Pat about going with me to the gun shop. Then I called Cole and I told him I wasn't coming in to work after all. It was time to be brave and do what I knew needed to be done.

chapter nine

Cole made me promise to wait on him to pick me up in his truck. He came to the door bearing gifts.

"Brought you a bagel and coffee," he said, handing me one of his own travel mugs full of homemade brew and a bag from Publix bakery.

"You're the best," I said, meaning it.

"Or the dumbest. What are we doing, Charlotte?"

"Well, I don't know about you, but I'm going to the shed to rescue Amber and Lily."

"I was afraid you were going to say that," Cole replied with a sigh.

"You don't have to come along."

"Yeah, I do. You'll never get that chain and lock off the door. I brought my bolt cutters."

I smiled at him. "Of course you did."

Cole and I arrived at Randy Tipton's property around seven-thirty, just as the sun was beginning to rise. He stopped the truck and hopped out to open the back. We grabbed the bolt cutters and the two pairs of waders he had pulled from his box of fishing gear. It took a few minutes to ourselves prepared, but once we hit the water we moved pretty quickly. Wading across was easier this time since we knew it was possible…and I wasn't freaking out over something brushing against my legs every few seconds.

Once we reached the other side, Cole rushed towards the door with the cutters. But, he stopped cold, staring at the door.

"It's unlocked," he mouthed, pointing the hanging chain like a mime doing an act.

We started to back away slowly, but the door swung open violently as Randy Tipton charged Cole and the two of them fell backwards. As I stepped towards them, Cole swung Randy to the side and wrestled him to the ground. They were both throwing punches when I ran past to get to Amber who was standing in the doorway.

"Come with me," I told her. "Where's Lily?"

"I'm here," replied the young girl, holding on to her mother's leg.

They followed me to the water's edge.

"You can wade across. It's not deep. Just hold on to each other," I told them. "I've got to help Cole. Go!"

I ran back towards the men, rolling on the ground still trading punches, and jumped on Randy's back. Wrapping my arms around him, I pulled back to remove him from atop Cole. But, I was no match for Randy's muscle and adrenaline. He threw me off his back and I hit the ground; my hip landing on a rock and sending a shock of pain throughout my body. Even though my efforts to remove Randy were a failure, I had at least managed to distract him enough for Cole to get in a solid punch and knock him to the ground. Randy's nose looked broken and blood was gushing from his nostrils. It only seemed to make him angrier. Cole looked at me with what seemed to be astonishment.

"Seriously?" He said as Randy rushed at him again.

Cole shoved me out of the way just before a right hook caught his jaw. He went sailing into the wall of the shed and wood splintered as he made contact. I winced and started to go help him but before I could move, Randy was already there and was drawing back to give Cole some more. Just as he got close Cole ducked and Randy hit the hard, wood wall. This time it was bones that were splintering. Randy screamed in agony but Cole didn't waste any time as he gave his opponent a forearm to the nose. This sent Randy through the door of the shed and onto the ground. He was out cold.

The two of us managed to get the broken door shut and locked it with the chain. Cole noticed my limping. He wrapped his arm around my waist and practically carried me through the water. I felt bad because he looked in a lot worse shape than me. Amber and Lily stood huddled near the truck, soaking wet and in a bit of shock.

"Are you two alright?" I asked them.

Amber nodded. "Who are you? How did you find us?"

"That's a long story," Cole replied. He reached in the truck, grabbed his cell phone and called the police. "We can tell you all about it while we wait for the authorities."

Sergeant Atwood was the first to arrive on scene. He was not, however, too thrilled with our recue.

"I don't know what made you think this was a good idea," he said first thing.

"You couldn't do anything. Your hands were tied," I told him.

"Tied by the law. Not enough evidence. No warrant," he stated.

"I know. That's why I took action. Because I knew you couldn't, and I knew it could be a long while before anyone else could get here."

"You two could've been killed. You could've gotten them killed," he exclaimed, motioning towards Amber and Lily.

"But, we didn't," I replied.

The sergeant huffed and gave Cole a look over. "You're pretty beat up."

"You should see the other guy," Cole quipped. The sergeant didn't laugh.

More officers arrived, and it wasn't long 'til we heard Randy banging on the shed door demanding to be released. He was sorely disappointed when two sheriff's deputies released him from the shed just to put him into handcuffs.

Standing together near the sergeant's car, Cole and I began to ask him questions.

"I don't get it," I admitted. "Why did Randy hold his own wife and daughter hostage?"

"From what we're piecing together, Amber had attempted to take Lily and leave the state when Randy hired his brother Roy to kidnap them and keep them locked up in that shed. His plan was to convince her to stay with him."

"Nothing says 'I love you' like being kidnapped and held against your will," Cole replied snarkily.

"After a couple of weeks, he realized his idea was flawed. But, he couldn't just let them loose. She would have reported him right away. So, he kept them in that shed; taking them food and supplies once a week. He held them at gunpoint off and on and even beat Amber a few times to make a point. Didn't take long for her to be so scared and intimidated that she wouldn't dare attempt an escape."

"Dear Lord. They're going to need a lot of therapy and support to get over this," I added.

"I'm glad they're safe and that he's going to jail, but there's still one piece of unfinished business we need to take care of," said Cole. "What started all of your amateur investigating in the first place...?"

"Oh! Yes! I need Amber to sign some paperwork concerning her guardianship rights of her nephew Maddox. He's up for adoption. Is there any way we could speak to her?" I pleaded.

"Come to the station and we'll get you a sit-down with her," the sergeant acquiesced.

"You go ahead," said Cole. "I'm going home to sleep another hour or so."

"Thank you, Cole," I told him, placing my hand on his arm. "You didn't have to support me like this."

"What are big brothers for?" he joked. He walked slowly towards his car, and then turned around. "By the way, I'm younger than you."

"What? Really?"

"By two years. Born in seventy-eight."

Ugh. I was born in seventy-six. "But, you're bigger than me so it still works," I yelled towards him as he continued to walk away.

"Yeah, whatever," he replied.

I arrived at the office just before noon. Thankfully, Cole had informed Mr. Baker of the morning's events.

"I assume you have paper signed," Mr. Baker greeted me as I walked in the door.

"Yes, Sir! She loves Maddox, but she's going to have her hands full getting herself and Lily settled into a new life. She wrote him a note that she would like for us to give his adoptive parents. They can choose whether or not to share it with Maddox."

"Excellent. I'm sure they'll be open to reading it at the very least. You did good, Charlotte. Not exactly work that fits your job description, but still…a good deed."

"Thank you, sir."

"You really helped the police find a missing woman and her daughter?" Ginny asked.

"Cole helped, too. That's what we were working on when we were away from the office. I brought you a little something as a thank you for putting up with our absences. You had to do a lot of extra work, and I appreciate it," I told her as I handed her a Starbuck's gift card.

"Thank you, Charlotte. That really means a lot."

I felt good. Peace had been made with Ginny.

"You know," she started, interrupting my moment of tranquility. "I didn't mind the extra work. I mean, I do this to help children. It's my gift! My passion! My husband makes a lot of money so I can do this sort of thing; you know, work for just a little over minimum wage. No wonder you aren't really dressed to the level of your position, Charlotte. A single woman with children can't be expected to survive on such minimal pay. Of course, I don't mind for myself because, well—"

"You're rich and it's your passion. We get it," snapped Cole. "I've got those forms you wanted. Come on, Charlie, we're going to lunch."

"But you just got here," whined Ginny.

"We all gotta eat," replied Cole.

"I'll come, too," said Mr. Baker. "I'm starved. Thank you, Ginny, for covering the office."

The three of us left and went to a local diner for burgers; not feeling one bit guilty about leaving Ginny there alone. Well, okay…maybe a little guilty. Fine, yes, we felt guilty so we took her a milkshake after we enjoyed our lunch. Geesh.

The day of Maddox's adoption was truly special. Mr. and Mrs. Murphy had been anxiously awaiting this day for some time. Everyone was happy and excited. Afterwards, the judge posed for pictures with the Murphys and their extended family which included Amber and Lily. None of us could have asked for a better outcome.

Randy Tipton and his brother Roy were behind bars, having plead guilty in hopes of leniency. Praying for them would be even more difficult than praying for Ginny. But, being a believer, I knew that praying for them would bring freedom to me—freedom from fear, bitterness, anger. I shared this belief with Amber; hopeful that she would find freedom, too. I teamed up with the Grannies to bless Amber and Lily with some love, prayer and baked goods. With those women praying for them, no doubt Amber and Lily would be just fine.

Y ou ready? Got everything you need?" asked Momma Pat.

"Yes, Granny Oakley. I'm all prepared," I teased.

We walked into Femme Fatale Arms, and I headed straight to the gun case.

"That's the one," I said, pointing to the Glock Gen 5.

"I knew it," said Marcy. "I knew when you left here the other day, you'd be back for that one."

"Good choice," said Momma Pat, smiling.

"And I want to sign up for the concealed carry class," I added.

Marcy nodded and went to get the appropriate papers. I turned around and surveyed the store, and a t-shirt caught my eye. It read:

P.M.S.

Pretty Mean Shot

I pulled a shirt from the rack and looked at it closely.

"And this. I'll take this, too."

Momma Pat laughed. "Another good choice!"

I had been sitting in the shade enjoying a cool breeze at the park, texting with Su about my week spent as a would-be investigator. She wasn't completely surprised that I had taken things so far. I did have to promise her I'd be more cautious should I ever want to pursue a rescue again, and she had to promise me phone call once her final exams were done.

Carrie, Joseph joined me at the covered picnic table, and we ate fried chicken from the Wal-Mart deli along with a shared large bag of generic potato chips. Tommy was busy going down every single slide on the playground.

"I know this is terribly unhealthy, but it's so good," Joseph said, with his mouth full.

"For real," added Carrie. "I'll make us all a salad for supper tonight."

Tommy came running up to the table. "Maymay! Today is the best! I love you!"

"Awww. I love you, too. In fact, I love you more than potato chips."

"I love you more than chocolate," Carrie said to Tommy.

"I love you more than pizza," Joseph told him.

Tommy giggled and smiled.

"And I love you more than coffee," I said. They all just stared at me.

"Okay, maybe not more than coffee. But, you're a close second."

The kids all laughed and Tommy ran off to play some more.

"Coffee and kids," I thought to myself, "definitely my two favorite things!"

the end

author's note

You can truly make a difference in the life of a child by becoming a Guardian ad Litem volunteer. For more information, visit guardianadlitem.org.

James 1:27

OTHER WORKS BY ALYSSA HELTON

DOGWOOD ALLEY

IF THE CRICK DON'T RISE

JOY IN THE MORNING

THE LION TAMER'S DAUGHTER

THE SUGARKING SHORTSTOP

Find exclusive short stories FREE for members at

www.alyssahelton.com

COMING SOON

BOOK TWO
OF THE CHARLOTTE RITTER MYSTERY SERIES

frappes, flamingos and a fireman

If you enjoyed this book, you may also like the Michael Tallen novel series. Let me introduce you to these stories with the introduction from the first book:

THE LION TAMER'S DAUGHTER

THE LION TAMER'S DAUGHTER

ALYSSA HELTON

THE LION TAMER'S DAUGHTER

Written by Alyssa Helton

ISBN-13: 978-1539882176
ISBN-10: 1539882179

INTRODUCTION

I approached the old home with its weathered siding yellowed by dirt and sunlight, and knocked on the rusty screen door. The door rattled and alerted a small dog inside who considered it his duty to bark incessantly until his owner hushed him with a swat from a rolled newspaper. A middle-aged man opened the door and looked me over head to toe before uttering a word.

"Can I help you?" he demanded.

"Yes, Sir. I'm Michael Tallen, a contributing writer with the Herald…"

"We already get the paper," he interrupted.

"Uh, no, Sir, I'm not selling the paper. I'm here to see a woman named Ruth who called our office. She didn't give her last name; just said she wanted a writer to come to this address to take down her story as her dying wish."

"Dyin' wish? She ain't dyin'! That woman will outlive us all," he exclaimed, shaking his head and pushing the screen door open to let me inside.

I stepped into the entry and the little dog, a yorkie, uttered a soft growl while he sniffed my shoes.

"That's Bruiser. She don't bite. Of course, I can't say the same for Ruthie," he told me with a raised eyebrow and a serious expression. "Somebody get Ruthie and tell her she has a visitor!"

"Quit calling me that, and get outta my way," demanded an elderly woman, walking our way with the aid of a cane. She had grey hair cut short and styled a bit like Helen Mirren, and wore jeans with a white button-up shirt along with a strand of pearls and ruby red lipstick. Not at all what I expected, I braced myself for her examination of my appearance and blunt disapproval.

"You must be the writer from the Herald. Come on in," she invited.

I admit I was a bit shocked. Usually one look at my long dark hair tied up in a "man-bun," my earrings and my tattoos; and people of a certain age would look at me with disgust and turn away. Not her. She didn't even flinch.

I followed her into a sitting room, and sat on an old, velvet couch that released a puff of dust and dog hair into the air.

"Can I get you somethin' to drink?" she asked as she sat in a recliner across from me.

"No, thank you. I was under the impression that having someone record your thoughts on your life was your dying wish, but the gentleman who answered the door indicated you're perfectly healthy."

"Well, I had to say something to get you here," she confessed. "I am eighty-nine years old, so I figure I'm closer to dying than most people. Call it 'creative truthing.'"

I chuckled and opened my notebook. I liked her spunk, and I figured anything she was so determined to say was worth recording.

"May I record this conversation?" I asked, pulling out my digital recorder.

"That's probably a good idea. We've got a lot of ground to cover. I can't expect you to memorize it all."

"A lot of ground, huh? Just what is it you're wanting me to write…your thoughts on life in general? A valuable lesson you've learned?"

"My story."

"Your story. As in your whole…life…story?"

"Yep."

I cleared my throat. "Ma'am, first of all, I write short articles for the Herald about the arts and community events. I'm not a biographer. Second of all, the newspaper isn't the proper medium for sharing one's life story. They won't even consider publishing it…"

"I know all that! I've followed your work for a long time."

"Yeah, exciting stuff, isn't it?"

"There's been times…regardless, I want YOU to write my story."

I shifted in my seat and attempted to gather my thoughts. How could I convince her this was a horribly bad idea?

"Ma'am,"

"Call me Ruth."

"Yes, m…Ruth. Uh…let's say I agree to write your story. Why is it so important to you to have it written? I mean, if you're wanting to pass down stories to your grandchildren, you could just have a family member write for you."

She stared at me with a slight grin, and we sat in awkward silence for a moment. I glanced around the room and noticed several framed black and white portraits in dusty, dark wooden frames. There were also what appeared to be framed newspaper clippings and photos of large animals, like elephants, hanging on the far wall. But, having forgotten to put in my contacts that morning, I couldn't make out any details.

"This isn't my house," she stated abruptly.

"It's not?"

"No. For the last fifteen years or so, this house was home to my dearest friend and cousin, Lizzie. We lived together as young girls on a farm in Ft. Lauderdale, not too far from here." She looked away, seemingly lost in thought. "She passed away this week. I came here for her funeral."

"I am so sorry. My condolences."

"Lizzie had kept boxes upon boxes of letters, pictures, and other odds and ends from our time together. I've been sifting through those precious memories, and well...I think there's a story to tell in it all."

She had me hook, line and sinker. I sat there not knowing anything about this woman; not even if she was telling the truth, but completely convinced I should write for her. Her wrinkled hands rested folded in her lap, and her emerald green eyes nearly stared right through me; looking at me with anticipation.

"Alright then," I began, turning on the recorder, "where do we start?"

She clapped her hands together and smiled, "From the beginning! Oh, but not here. Let's go down the hall to Lizzie's room with all the boxes."

Grabbing her cane, she was up and walking, leading the way to the room full of memories. We stepped inside a small bedroom wallpapered in a pale yellow floral print reminiscent of a Chintz china pattern my grandmother once had. A white metal bed covered in an antique quilt sat against the middle of the back wall. A well-worn wingback chair sat near the window. A simple wooden dresser stood in a corner, and boxes of various sizes, including a few old, round hat boxes, were scattered throughout the room. A few boxes remained sealed, but most of them were open and their contents spilling out onto the bed or the floor.

"Pardon the mess. As I go through each box, my mind wanders to other times and far-away places, and I lose track of time…and any motivation to clean this stuff up."

"It's fine," I assured her, as I perched on the edge of the bed and picked-up a random photograph. It was a photo of a young girl, a teenager, with long hair tied with a ribbon, and holding a large feather in one hand. "This looks like it's from the late thirties, early forties, I'm guessing."

"Let me see." She took the photo from me and sat in the chair by the window. "Ah, yes. I was fourteen. So, that would be…um…nineteen and forty-one. Oh, yes, that's it…nineteen forty-one." She handed me back the picture.

"I can see it now…the cheekbones, the eyes."

"I'm a long way from that girl, now."

"Nah. She's still there. I see her."

She grinned, and I think she even blushed a little.

"Let's start here," I suggested. "Tell me about this picture, about you at fourteen, and about this feather."

Ruth leaned back in the chair and closed her eyes, and for a brief moment I thought she may had fallen asleep.

"Feathers have always been my favorite, and that one was a real prize. It was a tail feather from a hawk. Cyrus, one of the snake charmer boys, had found it and given it to me. I begged my mother to make me a sequined headband and attach the feather, but she refused. She didn't want me to look like the other girls around camp."

"Whoa, whoa, wait a minute. Snake charmer? Girls at camp?"

"Oh, I didn't tell you?"

"I don't think so. Tell me what?"

"I was the lion tamer's daughter!"

After Ruth's exciting and rather bizarre revelation, she excused herself to "fetch a pot of tea" for the two of us. I slouched in my chair and surveyed the boxes of letters and pictures while questioning my sanity for remaining in the midst of such chaos. This poor, delusional, old woman was intent on holding me hostage to listen to her ramblings about a fictional world. Or maybe not. Maybe she was telling the truth.

I grabbed the box closest to me, and reached inside; blindly grabbing whatever rested near the top. Submitting to my grasp were three photos and a folded letter. The first photo showed its age with muted tones and worn edges; and pictured a teenage boy with a thin face and straight, dark hair. He wore a long-sleeved shirt with ruffles down the front, tights and what appeared to be ballet shoes that rested on the back of an elephant. Quickly turning the photograph over, I read a penciled inscription on the back, "Albert, 1941."

The other photos were of random people. They could have been friends or family, anyone really. And, I didn't dare read a personal letter without her consent. I stared at the picture of Albert, and realized Ruth might just be telling the truth…and it might be an amazing story that's worth hearing…and writing.

Ruth hobbled into the room shakily carrying a tray with a small tea pot and two cups with saucers. I swiftly rose to take the tray from her, and cleared a spot on the bed to set it down.

"I brought milk and sugar just like Maggie taught me when I was a girl."

"Who's Maggie?" I enquired as I discreetly pressed the record button on my digital recorder.

"She was one of the show girls, and she came all the way from London! She wasn't terribly talented, but she was beautiful, so Mr. Lewis found her a spot with the acrobats. She mostly stood and smiled and waved her arms about to direct the crowd's attention to what the acrobats were doing. Sweet girl. She made good tea."

Ruth poured tea into our cups and allowed me to add sugar and milk to mine as I pleased.

"I think we're getting ahead of ourselves," I paused the recorder. "So far you've told me your father was the lion tamer, there was a girl from London in the show, and some man named Mr. Lewis was apparently in charge. This story is all over the place...mind starting from the beginning?"

"Not at all!" she replied as she leaned back in her chair, holding her cup and saucer in her trembling hands.

"Oh, and I definitely want to know who this is," I told her, handing her the photograph of Albert.

"Albert!" she exclaimed with a smile as she looked upon the photo. "You will most definitely hear about him!"

"Good. Alright then. Where are we starting? Year? Location?" I took the recorder off pause.

"Hmmm. Well, this may be the best place to start right here; where this picture of Albert was taken. It was 1941 in Bradentown, on our way to Sarasota."

"I believe you mean Bradenton," I corrected.

"No, I don't. I mean Bradentown, as it was called since 1903. It wasn't until 1943 that the state of Florida merged it with another town, and called it Bradenton."

Sharp as a freakin' tac. She got me. I cleared my throat.

"I stand corrected," I said, apologetically. "Please continue."

She took a long sip of her tea. "As I was saying," she said, giving me a certain look. "We were camped in Bradentown. It was summer, and oh so hot…"

CONTINUED IN…
THE LION TAMER'S DAUGHTER

Made in the USA
Columbia, SC
05 June 2021